# The
# DESPERATE
# Deal

## DINEEN MILLER

VINCI
BOOKS

## By Dineen Miller

Seashells and Sunsets

*The Desperate Deal*

*The Friendly Disaster*

Messy Love on Mango Lane

*Bloomed to be Messy*

*Rescued to be Messy*

*Tamed to be Messy*

*To my husband Mike,*
*whose love rescued me and still does.*

Vinci Books

vinci-books.com

Published by Vinci Books Ltd in 2026

1

The publisher and the author have made every effort to obtain permissions
for any third party material used in this book and to comply with copyright
law. Any queries in this respect should be brought to the attention of the
publisher and any omissions will be corrected in future editions.
A CIP catalogue record for this book is available from the British Library.
Paperback ISBN: 9781036709372

The EU GPSR authorised representative is Logos Europe, 9 rue Nicolas
Poussion, 17000 La Rochelle, France
contact@logoseurope.eu

# Chapter One

How could one person's future teeter on the actions of another?

Sheridan Lane Scott turned down a side street, admiring the modest homes. Most were bigger than what her condo had been but nothing much compared to her parents' former residence.

But still, she'd be lying if she didn't admit she missed the security—and cleanliness—of her condo. Thanks to her father's embezzlement scandal, she had the pleasure of residing at the only place an unemployed, former socialite could afford—a seedy hotel on the outskirts of downtown Sarasota.

But her car—her one and only possession left from her former life—would live on a nearby street, safe from vandalism. Though most of what she had left in life now resided in a storage unit, she refused to let go of the little wine-red Jag her father had gifted her. The Feds had taken her condo, even though she paid the mortgage, but her car—that they could not touch.

1

She parked at the end of the street in front of a typical Florida stucco house. Before getting out, she swapped her business heels for a pair of jogging shoes. Another failed interview. No one wanted to hire her once they figured out who she really was. Even with the changes she made to her hair, her face was still too recognizable in the corporate world. She walked up to the door and rang the bell.

The top of Mr. Hodges' gray head appeared in the upper window as he peeked through the hole. He opened the door. Still in his bathrobe at noon meant he'd had a rough night.

"Hi, Sheridan."

She held out the envelope containing forty dollars. "Hey there, Mr. Hodges. Having a rough day?"

He shrugged as he took the envelope. "Not so bad." He held up her payment. "Thanks. This will help."

She raised a brow at him. "Don't buy too many donuts, okay?"

He smirked and nodded before closing the door.

At least she had a safe place for her car for another week. She walked the half-mile to her hotel, preparing herself for Jimmy's rancid breath and attitude. Even the heat and humidity of early afternoon couldn't ward off the shiver that came with her dread. The man made her skin crawl, which went well with the cockroach infestation she shared the place with.

One big happy family.

Not.

She rounded the shaggy bush at the sidewalk leading to the main office. At the door, she inhaled as much of the beach-scented air as she could to ward off the stink she was about to walk into.

Jimmy rose from his seat behind a desk that had probably looked great in the eighties and complemented his attire. The man was a leering cliché. "Well, hello there, gorgeous."

"Hi, Jimmy." She kept her smile in place. Her years in marketing and handling quite a few male egos had given her some skills to deal with the likes of him. "Here's my payment for the week."

He took the envelope, glanced inside, and pushed it back. "Yeah, that won't be enough."

"But that's what we agreed upon."

Held his hands out. "It's tourist season. Rates went up. What can I tell ya?"

"You can tell me you'll honor what we agreed upon."

"I wish I could, sweetheart, but I don't make the rules."

"That's not what you said when I moved in. You said you were in charge."

Her comment seemed to catch him off guard, but he rallied by holding his hands out and giving her a condescending glare. "Of the premises. Not the rules."

She blew out a frustrated breath and pushed the envelope back. "Okaaaaay, then how much time will this buy me?"

He looked inside again. "A day and a half...maybe."

"What?! Come on. That's too steep of an increase. Not good for business."

"And yet, folks are payin' it. You can always look elsewhere."

Jimmy wasn't in a negotiating mood. She'd have to find somewhere else to crash tomorrow. Maybe her best and last friend in the world would let Sheridan use her couch for a night or two. But today she had a job interview to get to.

She nabbed a twenty out of the envelope so she could at least buy something to eat later and slapped the rest on the counter. "That should cover me through tomorrow morning. And I want clean towels. Clear?"

His eyes traveled up and down her form as his mouth twisted into a leer that gave Jim Carrey's role as the Grinch a run for his money. "Towels...sure thing."

Sheridan headed back to her room to change clothes for her next interview. Too bad she didn't have time for a shower. After that encounter with Jimmy, she needed one.

And what did a greeter at an average restaurant wear? She'd frequented most of the higher-end places on Main Street, but Madilyn's Grill & Wine Bar hadn't really entered her radar nor the crowd she used to run with. Pineapple Avenue wasn't her usual hang out.

At this point, she'd take any job. Her marketing position at her father's company made her a hot potato for Sarasota's corporate world. At least until the talk died down and her father was proven innocent.

Hopefully...

---

The sound of dishes crashing blasted his ears as Noah Kent neared the kitchen. He launched into a run, then skidded to a stop at the edge of a puddle of red sauce. "What in the world?"

Chef Margot stood by a steel prep counter, eyes wild like a cow about to be slaughtered. He'd known Margot for years and had only seen her this rattled one other time— right after her mother's sudden death.

Sous-chef Manny stood by her, looking nearly as disturbed. Marinara sauce covered the front of his white jacket. "It's my fault. I spilled Chef's sauce."

Noah thumbed in the direction of the break room. "Go get cleaned up. I'll handle this."

Margot exhaled and slumped into herself. "I'm sorry. I know it was an accident. It's been a really, really rough morning." She gestured with one hand holding a rolling pin and the other a clump of dough.

Noah went around the prep counter to approach her from the other side. "Fill me in."

Giant tears welled up in her eyes and poured down her cheeks. "Gary left."

"Oh, man. I'm so sorry."

She buried her face against his shoulder, sobbing. "He doesn't even want to talk about it." She leaned her head back. "Six months! I gave him six months of my life." Her wild-eyed look had returned.

When she dropped her head against him again, he rubbed her shoulder, not knowing whether to ask for details or just let her cry. Gary hadn't seemed intimidated by Margot's rough and tough exterior. Quite the opposite—an ideal match. But what did he know?

Maybe he should give her the day off and let Manny handle things. Weeknights usually had lighter crowds, but the tourist season had definitely started earlier than normal. "If you need the night off, just say the word."

She stepped back with a hiccup. "No, I'd just be miserable at home."

She seemed pretty miserable now. And maybe a tad stressed—she gripped the dough so tight her fingers disappeared.

"Manny can handle things tonight and I can help."

She drew her brows together. "You?"

"Yeah, I've helped in the past."

"Yes, and as I recall, that did not go well. I'm fine." She

started slamming the dough on the counter to work the gluten. Rough and tough Margot had returned.

Noah headed back to his office. As he sat down, his cell phone buzzed—his weeknight greeter who had a habit of calling in sick lately. Oh goody. "Hi, Kelly. How ya doin'?"

"Not so good." She croaked her words but he could have sworn he heard a giggle in the background. "I won't be able to work tonight. Sorry."

"I understand. Take as much time as you need and call me when you feel better so I can give you your schedule, okay?"

"Um, okay."

He ended the call and put his cell on the desk, face down. Just out of high school—he predicted she would call in a few days when she ran out of money, or she wouldn't call at all. He sat back in his chair with a long sigh. Made a note on his desk calendar to mark her file 'terminated.'

Dressed in a fresh jacket, Manny paused in his doorway. "Rough day already?"

Noah popped forward in his squeaky chair, shifting the mouse to wake up his computer. He still had an order to complete. "You could say that. Be prepared to step in for Margot tonight. And I probably won't be able to help because we don't have a greeter for tonight. At least not yet."

"Kelly called in sick again?"

"Yep, but I don't think she'll be calling again."

He made a circle with his mouth. "You fired her?"

"Nope, just know how these things tend to work out. Besides, I have someone coming in today to interview for the weekend greeter position. Maybe she can start tonight."

Manny gave him a thumbs up before ducking out to return to the kitchen.

At least his core team proved dependable. Even on a bad day, Margot knew how to keep her kitchen running. And Manny's quick learning had landed him the role of sous-chef in record time.

Now if he could find a stable greeter, maybe he could concentrate on growing the business. His phone buzzed again. He ran his hands over his face before turning over his phone.

Jordan Lancaster's name showed on the screen. As an angel investor, the man's interference ran more on the devilish side. Especially since his daughter Sara had broken things off with Noah last year.

Another lesson learned. The hard way. Never mix business and pleasure.

Never, never, never.

He turned the phone back over. Lancaster would have to wait.

## Chapter Two

She strode down Pineapple Avenue, rehearsing for her interview. If Sheridan didn't land this job, she'd have to figure out a way to convince Jimmy to let her stay longer. A shiver jerked her words so she started over. "Hi, I'm Sheridan Lane. Hello, my name is Sheridan Lane. Pleased to meet you. Hi! I'm Sheridan Lane. Social outcast and desperate. Please hire me."

An older woman heading toward her stopped, hesitated, then shook her head as she continued. Sheridan resisted the temptation to stick her tongue out at the woman. Instead, she lowered her voice and continued to practice.

Each time, she emphasized 'Lane' to train her mind. If she gave her real last name, they'd tell her to leave before she had a chance to say anything else. No one in town wanted anything to do with the Scott family, guilty or innocent. So she would use her middle name for now. And hold her thumb over her last name if she had to show her driver's license.

That could work, right? She snorted to herself, drawing another concerned glance from a passerby.

She had to figure out something fast. Her family's fortune now lay in locked accounts, which included her trust fund. And unless her father's crack team of lawyers proved his innocence, they'd never see a penny of it again. While her father sat in prison, her mother had fled to Naples to stay with her sister until the trial. Which left Sheridan to fend for herself now that she no longer had a job at her father's company. Short of pawning a bauble or two, she had nothing left to her name, except her little car and she'd sell what little jewelry she had left before selling her car.

She believed her father—wanted to believe in his professed innocence. No way could Randall Scott have done such unscrupulous things, like swindling retirees out of their nest eggs.

Could he?

No, she refused to believe that the man who'd looked out for her every need—and wants at times—could be capable of such a thing. But the evidence…the FBI had taken everything, even her condo since her father had co-signed to help her get the mortgage loan. Granted, her salary had come from working for her father as a marketing analyst but that didn't mean squat at the moment. And she'd worked hard for her income. Her father had made sure of that.

She stopped short of the restaurant windows, closed her eyes, and inhaled. The embarrassment of it all still crushed her. She'd changed her name, lightened and cut her hair, and shed her designer clothes to conceal who she really was. Though Sarasota wasn't as large a city as other major metropolises, it still had a very active social scene. One in which she'd prided herself a key part.

Until now…

The hostess position in this restaurant would suit her if they'd give her a chance. She had a list of other jobs to try for if they didn't, but those paid much less and required some kind of uniform, which gave her a slight shiver too. But she'd do whatever was necessary to survive.

Composed and with a smile on her red lips, she pulled her shoulders back and strode into Madilyn's Grill & Wine Bar for her interview. After her eyes adjusted to indoors, she approached a man sitting in a booth with papers strewn on the table and a notebook in front of him where he made notes on what looked like a hand-drawn spreadsheet. Didn't he know you could download those things now and print them?

He wore a white linen button-down, open at the neck with the sleeves rolled up. He seemed too tanned and fit to be the manager—maybe an assistant. She'd frequented enough restaurants around town to know quite a few of the managers, and this guy didn't fit the usual persona of pasty and overworked. With Tourist Season in full swing, the snowbirds would be in town for at least a couple more months. And she needed a job, fast.

After what seemed a lifetime, he raised his head and gave her a rather annoyed look with eyes that matched the sea-green glass pendant light hanging over the table. Quite the contrast with his almost jet black hair. "Yes? May I help you? We're not open yet."

She swallowed the lump in her throat and stuck out her hand. "Hi, I'm Sheridan Lane. I have a greeter for the position interview."

Noah Kent lifted a brow, waiting for her to realize she'd jumbled her words. He'd expected someone younger for the interview, like a college student or even another high schooler. Not the polished woman who stood in front of him. Yet something about her seemed familiar...

She jerked her arm back, shook her head, and stuck her hand out again. "I mean, I'm Sheridan Lane. I'm here to interview for the greeter position."

Still holding his pen, he gestured to the booth seat across from him. "Have a seat and we'll get started."

She tugged her oversized purse in front of her as she sat. Sunlight streaming in from the front window caught the highlights in her honey-toned hair. "You're the manager?" She glanced at his shirt, looking for a name tag or something, he guessed.

He tilted his head. Was that disbelief he heard in her voice? "Yeah, you could say that." He held out his hand. "Noah Kent."

She shook his hand. "I guess I was expecting someone, you know, older."

He chuckled softly. "That's funny. I was expecting someone younger."

Her smile slipped a bit. She pulled a folder out of her bag and opened it on the table. "Here's my résumé." She held out a white sheet that had her name in large letters across the top.

Noah scanned the front before flipping the page over to see her qualifications continued there as well. "You seem a bit overqualified for this job, Miss Lane."

"I know, but I really need a job. And I have a lot of experience dealing with people. As you can see from the accounts I managed."

He looked at her resume again, catching the corporation name she worked for. "You worked for Serenity Group Investments? Didn't they just get shut down?" He regretted his words right away when she flinched.

She blinked several times before dropping her chin. "Um, yes, and why I really need this job."

Now he felt like a heel. He hadn't meant to upset her with his observation. But he had a bad habit of pointing out the obvious at times. Or so he'd been told. He gave her resume another pass to give her time to bounce back and him the time to figure out if he could hire her without his only reason being that he felt sorry for her. There had to be something she was good at that he needed right now, besides a pretty face, and that she most certainly had. Tourist Season had hit hard and fast after a painfully slow summer, which would allow him to implement some new ideas he had for the restaurant.

"The greeter position is part-time and only in the evenings. Could you take on some other tasks during the day?"

Her head shot up. "Like what? Washing dishes?" Her frown told him how she felt about manual labor.

He chuckled. "No, more along the lines of what you've done in the past." He spanned the restaurant with his gaze, taking in the quaint settings of the ornate bar, intimate booths, and cafe tables. "I want to create a social media presence for this place and add some events as well. Think you could help me with that during the day?"

Her eyes shone again with moisture, but her smile spoke her answer before she did. "Yes! I'd be great at that." Her eyes became circles to match her cute red lips. "I mean, I can totally handle that."

"Good. Then you're hired. You can start your hostess

hours tonight if you're available. And I want some marketing ideas in writing by the end of the weekend."

"I'll have pages of them." She slid out of the booth and grabbed her giant purse.

Noah tried to catch his glass of water in time, but not fast enough. Water dumped all over his spreadsheets and down his shirt.

"Oh, I'm so sorry!" Sheridan grabbed two cloth-wrapped silverware bundles off a nearby table and dumped the cutlery out with a crash before dashing back to soak up the water with the napkins.

Ink smeared across his spreadsheets. He snatched them up to shake off the excess water and to keep the napkins she wielded from making them worse.

She went to grab more bundles.

Noah reached out to catch her elbow but caught her hand instead. "It's okay. I'll take care of the rest."

She bounced her gaze to where their fingers tangled and then back up to his.

Noah meant to move a little quicker…a bit faster, but something vulnerable in her eyes threatened to grab hold of the soft spot in his chest. He slipped his hand from hers.

"So sorry for the mess." She pulled her purse straps over her shoulder.

"Don't worry about it. Be back here at three-thirty."

Her smile returned, lifting her cheeks to accent the tilt of her dark brown eyes. "Thank you."

She walked to the door, then stopped and turned around. "Um, just one question."

Noah grabbed a bar mop from the greeter stand near the door. "Shoot."

"What should I wear?"

# Chapter Three

Well, at least she'd gotten her name right. Sheridan breathed a small sigh of relief. Something had gone her way for once. Could she hope that things might finally go her way and life would have some semblance of normalcy again soon?

She had exactly two hours before she started her first hostess shift at Madilyn's Grill. Which meant she had an hour to find a pair of black slacks in her storage unit, get back to her hotel, and change. Sheridan pulled down another box and pulled open the flaps.

Bingo! Black slacks and a red paisley silk top to boot. She glanced at a clear container that held some of her designer shoes, including a pair of red Jimmy Choo heels that would complete her ensemble to perfection, but that wasn't going to happen. She'd stick with her nondescript black wedges. Noah has suggested black slacks and shoes but left the top up to her.

Traffic seemed to give her a break for once and gave her a clear road to her hotel—her car wouldn't be there long enough to invite attention. And that would give her extra time to sweep her hair up too. As she pulled into the space in front of her unit, Jimmy walked down the sidewalk toward her, but he didn't appear his usual friendly and leering self.

She got out of her car and shot to her door but he'd anticipated her move and blocked her way. "Can't let you do that, sweetheart."

Sheridan jerked back. "I paid you for the day."

"It's Tourist Season. We strictly rent by the hour now."

She glanced at her watch. "I have twenty hours left."

"Rates went up."

"But we had an agreement, Jimmy." She clutched her pants and purse closer. For once she wished her instincts had been wrong, but she'd suspected a low life like Jimmy would pull a stunt like this. He'd made his intentions clear from the beginning. "I start my new job in an hour, so I can give you the difference when I get paid next week."

He snatched the key card from her hand. "Next week? Sorry, love. Can't do that. I need the room. Your stuff is by the dumpster. If it's still there." He laughed as he walked away.

She growled and stomped her foot. As she dashed around to the back of the hotel, a homeless man stood by what she recognized as her suitcase. "Hey, that's mine!"

The man slipped on her favorite fuzzy robe before grabbing more of her stuff and dashing off.

She rushed over to the decimated remains of her suitcase, whose contents spilled out like a gutted wild boar. Or so she imagined based upon what she remembered one of her father's hunting buddies describing.

Movement in her peripheral vision caught her attention. The homeless guy peeked around a dumpster about fifty feet away, most likely making sure she didn't leave anything. "It doesn't fit you by the way!"

He ducked behind the green behemoth he probably called home. She could chase after him, but then she'd be a mess for her new job. She'd have to make do with what she had left. Sheridan shoved as many items as she could salvage back into her suitcase. Her favorite eye shadow palette lay in a shattered mess along with the remains of her favorite perfume bottle. Jimmy knew how to hit a girl hard without touching her.

She loaded her few belongings into her car and drove back downtown. Later she'd figure out a place to sleep for the night, but first, she needed to get ready for her shift. She'd noticed a cute clothing shop two doors down from Madilyn's when she left earlier. Maybe she could slip in there and change.

After parking in the lot behind the restaurant, she hoofed it to Pineapple Avenue. She had less than a half-hour before she had to clock in. A couple of people stood browsing the bathing suit racks at Sass & Sun Fashions, so she made her way toward the back, picking up a top to try on so she'd blend in better. The only salesperson she identified in the store seemed to have her hands filled with one customer trying on several items.

Sheridan pulled the curtain closed behind her, hung the blouse she had no intentions of trying on the hook, and pulled her black slacks and a red and black, tie at the waist blouse out of her oversized purse. She kicked off her shoes and slipped on the new outfit.

A voice came from outside of the curtain. "Hon, you need any help in there?"

"No thanks. I'm almost done." Sheridan swept her hair up and grabbed a clip from her purse. She pulled a thick strand out on each side to compliment her silver drop earrings.

After strapping her shoes back on, she shoved her clothes into her bag, grabbed the hanging blouse, and pushed back the curtain.

A sales clerk she hadn't noticed when she came in stood in the middle of the dressing area, rehanging articles of clothing from a stack of hangers that cascaded to the floor. She pointed to the blouse Sheridan held with a hanger. "Did you like the fit on that one? I've had several customers tell me the hanger doesn't do it justice."

Sheridan held it out to her. "No, I think I'll pass. Thanks."

The sales clerk took the blouse, tilting a head full of long braids. "I don't recall you wearing that outfit when you came in."

Sheridan's heart raced up a notch. She glanced down at her attire. "Oh this, I had it in my bag already. To be honest, I just needed a place to change. I start a new job at Madilyn's in," she checked her watch, "five minutes. Yikes, I should go."

The clerk stopped her with a hanger. "Hold on there, chickadee. I'm sure you can understand that I need to do my due diligence."

Sheridan felt her pulse pounding in her neck. If the clerk didn't believe her, she'd be late and out of a job unless Noah Kent gave her a break. And she didn't seem to be getting very many of those these days. "I swear, these are my clothes."

"Open the bag, please."

She yanked her bag off her shoulder and opened it.

The clerk used the hanger she still held to push things

around. "Yep, that's the outfit you had on when you came in."

"Then you believe me?"

"Not yet. Let me see the tags on those pants."

"Fine." She spun around, pulling the waistband out so the clerk could see the label. "I seriously doubt you carry this brand here."

The clerk made a face at her. "Well, aren't you Miss Snotty Pants. Evelyn, grab Hank from outside. We may have a shoplifter here."

"What? No, I'm sorry. Seriously, these are my clothes. I just needed a place to change. That's all."

A burly man around the age of fifty shuffled in. Not a cop but definitely security. "What seems to be the problem, Kaleena?" He held the front of his wide belt like the cops she'd seen on television shows.

"Little Miss Snotty Pants here might be trying to pull one off on us."

How would she get out of this one? She held her hands out. "I confess I used a dressing room to change clothes. That's all. I showed her my pants label." She dropped her bag on the floor and then tugged the collar of her shirt around. "Here's the label from my top. I'm pretty sure the shop doesn't carry this brand either."

He leaned in, looked, then raised his brows at the clerk. "Kay?"

She pursed her lips, which pushed her nose up. "No, we don't carry either one."

The security guard nodded, returned his hands to their place on his belt. "All right then, I see no problem here." He gave Sheridan a piercing look. "Ma'am, I suggest you change your clothes at home next time."

Sheridan bent over to grab her purse and mumbled to herself. "I would if I had one." As she straightened, she dared a look at the clerk who stood with her arms crossed and a deep frown on her face. "I'm so sorry. I just really need this job."

The woman's features softened a bit. She waved a hand toward the door. "Go on, get going."

Sheridan raced out onto the sidewalk and toward the restaurant. No time to put her bag in her car. She yanked open the door and barreled inside. Her brain registered Noah standing there with a bottle of wine in his hand, but not in time to stop her forward momentum. Then everything seemed to shift into slow motion, like the slapstick comedies her friend Emma binged on after a break-up.

The bottle flew out of Noah's hands.

She tried to reach for it just as he did.

The bottle spun, splashing red wine across his white shirt.

As she fell on her rump on the floor, she cringed at the crash of glass.

She groaned. What a way to start a shift, splattered on the floor with a bottle of wine.

Noah surveyed the mess. "Don't move. There's glass all around your feet."

He ran to the back to get what she imagined could include a firing squad. She'd organized enough of her parent's social events to know that about two hundred dollars of wine now sat in a puddle around her feet.

Noah came back with one of the kitchen staff, who began sweeping the glass into a dustpan. The rich aroma of the red wine filled her nose as Noah helped her up.

"I'm so sorry. I was running to get here on time…" She

touched the stain on his shirt, then jerked her hand back, realizing she'd touched him. "I, uh, I will pay for that to be cleaned."

*Just please don't fire me.* She held her breath, waiting for him to tell her to leave.

And judging by the expression on his face, she'd be walking out of the place within seconds—she glanced down —with sticky feet and squeaky shoes. "Oh, no."

Noah grabbed a stack of bar mops and a spray bottle from the hostess stand before crouching in front of her. "Hold on to the stand."

He lifted one of her feet and unstrapped her shoe. The warmth of his hand on her ankle did weird things to her pulse, but the way he carefully wiped her foot and cleaned her shoe made her want to cry. Then he put her shoe back on and even buckled it before moving on to her other one. So caring and gentle.

Almost intimate.

She leaned over, catching the earthy scent of his cologne. *Or was that just him?* She fought the sudden urge to run her fingers through the dark sweep of hair that had fallen across his forehead.

Once finished, he stood. "There's a mop and bucket in the back. Ask Manny if you can't find it."

She couldn't move, couldn't find her voice over the lump lodged in her throat. Nor could she tear her gaze away from him. Every detail of his face, from the inset of his ocean-like eyes set deep under full black brows to his angled jaw that highlighted well-defined lips now burned in her memory with an unexpected attraction and...something akin to affection.

He tilted his head. "Are you sure you're okay?"

She swallowed and nodded. "Yes. Manny. Mop."

Could she be any more pathetic? She dashed toward the kitchen like a shy schoolgirl who'd just met her first crush.

A green-eyed, black-haired knight in a wine-stained shirt that she never saw coming.

---

Noah shook his head as she scurried toward the kitchen. He'd opened the wine to let it aerate in anticipation of Lancaster's visit tonight. A two hundred dollar bottle to boot.

The sound of the mop bucket rolling and sloshing announced her return. Small puddles marked her path. He squelched down a grimace. This would be a long night of training. He just hoped Sheridan Lane would be worth his time.

He took the mop from her. "I'll get this. Go finish cleaning up. We open in thirty minutes and I still have to show you the ropes."

She scanned the restaurant.

He pointed toward the right side of the bar. "Restrooms are down the hallway."

Her shoes squeaked as she walked away.

Noah ran the mop several times over the floor and under the entry mat, which had soaked in a fair bit of the wine. "That's gotta go." He rolled up the mat and took it to the back. When he returned, Sheridan had the mop going again, catching the additional puddles she'd created the first go-round.

"There. All done." She pushed the mop into the bucket, causing pink water to slosh onto the floor. "Sorry!" She grabbed another bar mop and soaked up the puddle.

One of the busboys came out from the back. Noah

called him over and asked him to take the mop, bucket, and sodden towels to the back. "Thanks."

Now to train Sheridan. He spent the next twenty-five minutes going over the seating charts, the staff assignments, and her other responsibilities, like making sure the tables and the seats got a good wipe down after the busboys cleared the dishes.

Sheridan seemed receptive and eager to learn the ropes. Once he completed each part of the instructions, she would repeat it back to him to make sure she had it down. She got the details right each time too, which impressed him. What she lacked in coordination she made up in determination. So far at least.

Their first reservation walked in just as he finished. She glanced up at him, appearing nervous as she ran her hands down the front of her slacks.

"Ready?" He lowered his head as he lifted his brows.

She gave him a tremulous smile and a quick nod.

"Okay, the show's all yours now, Sheridan Lane."

Noah made a quick exit to his office to find a clean shirt. Fortunately, he picked up his dry cleaning across the street before he came in. He buttoned the fresh shirt as fast as he could and tucked the tails in on his way back to the front. They had a few reservations for the evening, but most of their business would come from walk-ins on a weeknight like tonight. Hopefully, Sheridan wouldn't have any more disasters.

His cell phone buzzed. A text from Lancaster telling him he wouldn't make it tonight. Too bad he hadn't texted sooner. That bottle of wine might still be in the rack and not down the kitchen drain. Just like Lancaster to change his plans at the last minute. Noah has witnessed it many a time while dating Sara. The man loved being in control.

Noah stopped where the hallway to the kitchen opened into the main dining area and stepped off to the side so as not to stop the steady flow of staff moving between the kitchen and the clientele. Sheridan held a stack of menus in her left arm, appearing like a schoolgirl, as she tilted her head toward a booth and seated another couple.

But the elegance she exuded with her hair pulled up and the curve of her hips as she leaned over to place menus in front of the guests screamed everything but schoolgirl. He pulled his attention to the other side of the restaurant to regain his composure. Sheridan had tapped into something deep within him in a very short amount of time.

Her movement in his peripheral vision brought his focus back to her though.

She met his stare and gave him a quick smile before returning to the front to greet a couple waiting to be seated.

He continued to observe her as she engaged with the guests and checked the reservation sheet on the podium. All smiles and graceful gestures, the woman knew how to handle people. That was obvious.

Margot walked up to him. "New girl seems to know what she's doing."

He glanced at her then continued to scan the room, careful not to stare at Sheridan but completely aware of her every movement. "Yeah, So far so good. She has a marketing background and may be able to help us there as well."

"Marketing? And she came in for the greeter position?"

He crossed his arms and leaned against the wall. "Yeah, she needed a job."

"Hmm, very interesting." Margot went back into the kitchen.

Very interesting indeed. He made a decision to keep his

23

guard up because Sheridan Lane intrigued and concerned him all at once.

Something about the woman just didn't add up.

# Chapter Four

The night had gone smoothly in her opinion. She'd tapped into every nuance of her professional experience to be the consummate greeter she sensed Noah wanted for his restaurant. From her observations, she could tell he cared not only for his restaurant but for the people who worked for him. He seemed very concerned about the chef, which made her wonder if something had happened.

And she hadn't missed the way he watched her throughout the evening. Purely professional, she was sure, but still, she had to admit she found herself searching for him throughout the night to see if he was there, watching her with eyes that made her want to dive into the depths of Noah Kent.

Almost felt like a game. Or a challenge. His constant presence exhilarated her but seemed to comfort her as well, as if he were her protector. Which made her feel empowered. She'd never met a man like him. Most seemed either threatened by her confidence or acted like a loyal puppy.

But that was the old Sheridan. She didn't want to be that woman anymore.

Although she did turn a bit red under the collar when he brought out a bottle of wine for a couple she seated. Noah had waited until she walked away to pour their samples. She'd have to prove to him that she wasn't a klutz all the time and that she knew how to ensure the clientele had a great dining experience. She'd managed most of her parents' dinner parties, so she had the experience. Too bad she couldn't tell him that though.

As she opened her locker to grab her purse, her mind flashed to the way he wiped the wine from her feet and shoes with such great care. Like an act of service or something. She felt humbled all over again by images of him crouched in front of her. And her ankles warmed, as if remembering the touch of his hands.

"You did great tonight."

She jumped, dropping her purse to the floor, and watched in horror as everything spilled out, including the baggie holding a spare bra and panties that she'd thrown in her bag. And there went the baggie with her toothbrush, toothpaste, and tampons.

The triple T! Could she crawl in her locker and hide?

Noah dropped to a crouch and began scooping the items back into her purse.

She lunged for the baggies, colliding with his hand at the same time.

His eyes captured and held her gaze. "Sorry, I didn't mean to startle you. I thought you heard me call your name."

"It's okay. I was thinking about the evening." She shifted her attention to the few remaining items on the floor, shoving them into her purse as fast as she could. With her life so up in the air these days, she carried her most basic items with her all of the time.

"How do you feel things went?"

She stopped and searched his face for some clear indication of how to answer his unexpected question. "Um, good, yes, I think." And why did she become a bumbling idiot around this man? "I mean, I think it went well." There, at least she sounded semi-literate that time.

He rose to his feet just as she did. "Great. Then I'll see you tomorrow evening." At the door to break room, he turned around. "And I'm looking forward to hearing your marketing ideas for the restaurant."

She smiled and nodded. "Can't wait."

Once he disappeared down the hall, she blew out a breath and sat on the bench in front of the lockers. She'd stood in front of corporate CEOs, confident and quick on her feet. Yet with this man, she felt like a silly schoolgirl with two left feet and a sudden case of the wallflowers. Something about Noah Kent pushed her off balance, bringing her klutzy side out in full force.

Sheridan pushed her tired body up from the seat and slung her bag over her shoulder. Without a credit card and no more cash, she had very few choices for the night. She'd texted her best friend Emma for a bailout but forgot that her parents were in town visiting for the week and sleeping on her lumpy fold out.

Her ex would probably help her, but he was in a new relationship, and no way would she cause more trouble for him. She'd done enough of that in the past. And most everyone else had snubbed her when the news broke about her father.

Tears burned her eyes as she thought about the direction her life had turned. She couldn't take anything for granted anymore and perhaps that was the blessing in disguise in all this. She just wished it didn't require sleeping in her car tonight. Maybe if Emma and her parents were going out for the day, she could use her shower to at least clean up in the morning.

She moved her little car behind the dumpster so as not to be too obvious. A few cars still speckled the back parking lot that several stores shared and backed up to a medical complex behind that.

After sending a quick text to Emma about using her shower in the morning, she reached behind her to grab a T-shirt from her suitcase. No point in sleeping in her good silk blouse all night. She tugged the bottom of her top up to pull it over her head and found herself stuck. Her blouse must have caught on something, and she couldn't move much without ripping it.

She grunted as she shifted her back end toward the door to lean over the center console. A sudden bright light shining in from the passenger side window blinded her, and its owner tapped on the window.

"Sheridan?"

She jerked up, ripping her blouse and smacking her elbow on the steering wheel. She yelped at the pain.

"Sheridan, are you all right?" Noah stared at her through the windshield as he put his phone down. He tried the door handle but she'd locked the doors.

She dropped her head back for a brief second, eyes closed and more embarrassed than she could ever remember being before opening her door and getting out. As she stood, she felt a rush of night air on her shoulder. When she glanced down, she saw that her blouse only covered one side of her chest, leaving her lacy red bra fully exposed.

Sheridan jerked up the corner of her top.

Correction...this was now *the* most embarrassing moment of her life.

---

Noah spun around to give Sheridan a moment to cover herself. He hadn't meant to startle her...again, but seeing the nose of a car peeking out from behind the restaurant dumpster had sent up warning flags. They'd had issues in the past with some shady activities in the parking lot, but then he'd recognized Sheridan behind the wheel.

He kept his back to her. "Let me know when you're decent."

Her soft sob met his ears along with the rustling of fabric. "You can turn around now."

She'd swapped her torn blouse for an oversized T-shirt that had the words 'This is my otter shirt' with a cute picture of the animal.

He tried not to grin but how could he resist when she stood there not only looking sad and pathetic, but adorable as well. He'd never met anyone like her. "What are you doing out here? Don't you have a place to go?"

She twisted one hand into the bottom of her shirt with the other. "If I tell you the truth, can I keep my job?"

Her question caught him off guard for a moment. "Unless you're doing something illicit, illegal, or deadly, the answer is probably yes."

She dropped her hands to her sides. "I unexpectedly lost my hotel room today and didn't have time to make other plans."

He pointed at the Jag. "Were you planning to sleep in your car?"

"Yes." She just stared at him, expressionless. The overhead lights made the tear tracks on her face glisten.

"Why were you staying at a hotel, if you don't mind me asking?" She drove a Jag and didn't have a place to live? What on earth had happened to this woman?

She leaned over to wipe her face with the bottom of her shirt. "I lost my condo."

"Because of what went down with Serenity Group?"

"Yes." Her reply came out as a rough whisper.

Noah walked around the back of the car to her side. "I'm so sorry, but I get it. My father lost everything he had, thanks to that scummy group."

She flinched at his words.

He did it again. "I'm sorry." He rubbed his forehead. "I'm didn't meant to imply anything—I know the case isn't settled yet. That was thoughtless of me. I'm sure you and your colleagues are as much the victims in all this as my father was."

She blinked several times. "I'm so, so sorry your father was hurt."

The emotion in her voice cut right into his chest. "Thanks. He's doing okay. I'm glad I'm able to help him."

"He's very fortunate to have you then."

He crossed his arms and leaned on the car. "What about you, Sheridan Lane? Don't you have a parent somewhere, or family who can help you right now?"

She shook her head. "No, they're in no position to help me at the moment."

"No friends?"

"Not at the moment." Now she sounded frustrated even to herself. "Listen, I really don't want—"

"Then you can stay with me." The words blurted out before he had time to really consider what he might be getting himself involved with. Or who. But how could he let her stay in her car for the night? Canned sardines had more room.

Her shocked expression shifted to confusion, or was that suspicion? "I don't know…"

He held his hands up. "I have no intentions here. I promise. Just trying to be helpful. I have a guest room you're welcome to use until you can make other arrangements."

"But you don't even know me." She drew her eyes together and pursed her lips. The clip holding her hair up gave way, causing her hair to tumble down onto her shoulders and around her face.

He dropped his gaze and resisted the temptation to find out what her hair felt like. Would it be as silky to the touch as he suspected? "I know, but my gut says you're just down on your luck and need a hand. We've all been there."

"You have?" She straightened from picking up the hair clip from the ground and looked at him as if surprised he could have hit a rough patch in life.

"Yes, several times actually." He held his hand out to her car. "Listen, you're welcome to stay in your car if you prefer. But—."

"No! I mean, thank you. Yes, please, I'd love to sleep in your bed. I mean a bed! In your room. Guestroom! And use your shower." She covered her mouth with her hand as if embarrassed. "Been a long day."

"And messy."

She laughed, which made him smile at the sound of it. Hearty, like somewhere in there lurked a woman who knew how to enjoy life when things weren't so difficult.

"I'm in that car there." He pointed to his red Tesla parked behind the back door of the restaurant. "Just follow me to the house. It's only about fifteen minutes away."

"Okay, thanks." Appreciating his taste in cars—and the color—she got back into her Jag.

As he pulled out of the parking lot, Noah checked his rearview mirror to make sure she was behind him. His therapist mother told him once he had a Messiah complex at times, and that only grief would come from such situations. He didn't know if he believed her but he never forgot what she said.

But for the first time, he truly hoped she was wrong.

## Chapter Five

The first glimmer of morning brought Sheridan out of her slumber. Took her a moment to remember she'd slept in her boss' guest room. Yesterday's events replayed through her thoughts like a blooper reel from a movie. She slapped her hands over her eyes in an attempt to make it stop and groaned. Today had to be a better day, right?

She'd make sure of it.

As the light grew brighter, she studied the simple furnishings of the room. The dark wood dresser with a mirror that didn't match. Neither did the nightstands. The bed creaked when she shifted, and the spread looked more like something her mother would have bought twenty years ago.

But she didn't care about any of that and actually found it cute. Noah clearly saw home decor in the light of basic necessities. Nothing more. Yet she found the picture he'd hung over the bed to be the most fascinating and telling of anything in the room.

She sat up in bed and twisted around to study the

painting better in daylight. And right side up. A woman stood at the threshold of a forest, facing the trees with her back to the viewer. A light from an unknown source illuminated the trees from behind and lit the path where she stood. The image was haunting and enlightening all at once. Depending upon one's perspective, Sheridan could imagine it being frightening for some and inspiring for others. Like the promise of possibilities. Or adventure. Or awaiting disaster...

She could describe her life at the moment as an adventure, which was way more hopeful than seeing it as a disaster.

From socialite to social pariah—she felt like Cameron Diaz in *The Holiday* with a narrator announcing the tagline of her life.

*Socialite to social pariah! Would Sheridan Lane get her life back together? And would it include a sexy—*

She sighed as she threw the covers off, swinging her legs off the side of the bed.

Creaks from the other side of the door and a knock launched her off the bed. She went to grab her robe from her suitcase but then remembered it now adorned a homeless man somewhere near downtown. She needed something to cover her shortie pajamas.

She pulled on an oversized, faded hoodie she'd had since she was a teenager and cracked open the door.

Noah stood holding a cup of coffee. "Good morning. I heard the bed creaking and figured you were up. There's coffee in the kitchen, so help yourself."

The brew from his cup wafted up her nose and jerked her brain to attention. She hadn't even run a brush through her hair yet, let alone brushed her teeth. "Thanks."

He lifted his cup to her and nodded before turning around.

Sheridan shut the door and checked her cell. Eight o'clock. She felt like a bum just waking up when Noah looked as if he'd already started his day hours ago. Didn't managers get to sleep later since they wound up working late most nights?

She better get in gear and start working on those marketing strategies he wanted. As much as she appreciated the room, being in close proximity to her boss felt like she was always on the clock. She had to find a place to stay and fast.

Grabbing clothes, she dashed into the attached bathroom and did a double-take. The band she used to tie her hair up at night had slipped, making the bun look more like a ragged fan. And apparently, she'd drooled in the night because she had a white crusty line down one side of her mouth. She refused to look anymore and dashed into the shower.

After she finished getting dressed, she made the bed but paused to study the painting again. The signature in the corner caught her eye this time.

N. Kent.

Had Noah painted it? The man was a vault of secrets she found herself wanting to crack. Although the one area she hoped to avoid was his father and his lost fortune. The thought twisted her very empty stomach into a knot of nausea.

She left her room and headed toward the sounds coming from the kitchen. And voices. Did Noah have company? She never thought to ask if he was in a relationship with someone. As she entered the kitchen, she put on a smile, ready to greet whoever lay in wait.

An older version of Noah sat at a cute round table with parlor chairs, like the ones at the restaurant.

Noah shut the refrigerator and stood by the man. "Dad, this is Sheridan. She'll be staying with us until she finds a place. Sheridan, this is my father, Norman."

Us? She darted her gaze between the two men staring at her, then extended her hand. "Pleased to meet you. And sorry to be in the way. I hope to be out of your hair as soon as possible." She bit her lip when she realized Norman was pretty much bald.

Noah patted his father on the shoulder. "You're not in the way at all. Right, Dad?"

"Not at all. Nice to have you here, Sheridan." He smiled at her as if she were some long-lost relative.

She swallowed the swirl of acid circling the drain of her guilty conscience. "Thank you."

Her stomach did another tumble, leaving her feeling queasy. She leaned on one of the chairs. What were the odds?

The sooner she found a place to stay, the better.

---

"Are you okay?" Norman Kent looked up at her with concern. "Noah, get the girl something to eat." He pushed out the chair next to him. "Sit and have some breakfast. When was the last time you ate?"

Noah studied her for a moment before bringing over the plate he'd intended for himself and set it in front of her. The faded jeans and oversized T-shirt knotted at the waist complemented her natural beauty. But he still liked that cute mass of hair she'd had when he first saw her this morning. She'd looked rather cuddly.

She rubbed her forehead as she sat down. "I don't remember to be honest."

Noah set a plate of scrambled eggs in front of her, garnished with chives and a side of bacon. Her stomach growled her thanks before she could. He chuckled. "I'm guessing it's been a while."

"Wow, that looks amazing. Thank you." She scooped a large bit of eggs into her mouth, moaned, and then covered her mouth with a shy glance. "Sorry, guess I was pretty hungry. Is that parmesan I taste in the eggs?"

Noah cracked two more eggs into his prep bowl. "Yes, and a touch of smoked paprika."

His father pointed at him with his fork. "That's his secret ingredient, smoked paprika. He puts it in everything."

"Dad, I do not put it in everything. Just most things." He poured more egg mixture into a frying pan and let them set a moment before stirring. Having his father around had taken some adjustment, but they'd eventually fallen into a comfortable routine after a month or so. And since his father had already retired for the night by the time he got home, he didn't have a chance to fill him in about Sheridan.

But her presence here didn't seem like an intrusion at all. Even his father seemed at ease with her, which he never did around Sara. Very interesting…

After prepping a new plate for himself, Noah joined them at the small table. When he scooted his chair in, his knees bumped Sheridan's, causing her to jump. "Sorry about that. I'm still waiting for the dining room set I ordered to be delivered."

"It's okay." She leaned over to look under the table. "Looks like the ones at the restaurant."

"It is. We had an extra so I borrowed it. But, when we expand to have more outdoor tables and lunch seating, it will go back. One of the many new features I'm adding to the restaurant."

She took a bite off of the slice of bacon she held and put it back on her plate. "Right! Just give me a sec." She jumped up from her chair and left the kitchen.

His father leaned over, his face a picture of mischief. "I say we keep her. Nice to have a lady around the house. Why don't you rent her the room and make it legit?"

"Dad, I'm sure Sheridan would prefer to find her own place."

He shrugged. "Just a thought."

Sheridan rushed back and sat down, holding a leather notebook and a pen. "I want to jot down what your goals are so I can start outlining some strategies."

"All right." He sat back, forming the list in his mind. "Outdoor dining, which will feature trivia on Wednesdays."

She puckered her face into a cute frown. "I wouldn't do Wednesdays."

"Why not?"

"You'll miss the church crowd. A lot of churches have events on Wednesdays, especially the more conservative churches. Why not Tuesday? That way Madilyn's will be more inclusive."

Noah nodded. He'd give her that one. "And karaoke on Fridays."

She stopped writing and met his gaze. "You sure about that?"

"What, you don't like karaoke?"

Crossing her arms, she sat back. "I did about ten years ago and only at the local bar joint. Madilyn's has a different crowd."

His father pointed his fork at her. "Exactly. I like this girl. She's smart."

Noah laughed. "Yes, Dad." He glanced at his watch and rose from his seat. "I have to go. Meeting a new vendor this morning. Can we finish this at the restaurant tonight? Maybe you could come a half-hour earlier. I can give you a printout of what I have in mind so far."

"Yeah, sure. No problem." She went back to jotting down notes in neat, capital letters with underlines to emphasize certain words.

He found himself lingering a moment, not wanting to leave. "Great, I'll see you later."

His father gave him a quirky, knowing grin. If his growing interest in Sheridan was that obvious, had she noticed it too? When he glanced at her again, she was munching on a piece of bacon in her left hand while she made notes with her other.

He shook his head at his father to send the message to let it go. Noah knew better than to mix business with pleasure, and his father knew exactly why.

# Chapter Six

Sheridan waited for Noah to leave before looking up. She didn't want to give any indication to his father that she regretted his son's leaving. How can she miss someone she just met?

Now she had to figure out how to disengage from Norman before her nagging guilt made her spill the beans about who she really was. She didn't like the idea of hiding the truth, but what choice did she have at the moment?

She finished the last of her eggs and gulped down the rest of her tepid coffee. "I should get going too. Lots to do today."

Norman put his hand over hers. "Take a moment to breathe, young lady. Take it from someone who knows... having the carpet yanked out from under you leaves you shaken and unsteady. I made the mistake of trying to fix everything by myself and wound up in the hospital with a mild heart attack. Let yourself recover a bit. Noah is in no rush to see you go. And neither am I."

And a heart attack...could this scenario get any worse?

Her throat closed to about a quarter of its usual size. Mouth dry, she worked her tongue loose from the roof of her mouth. She repeated what she said to Noah the night before. "But you don't even know me."

"No, but my gut tells me you're a decent person in need of help. We've all been there."

"That's what your son told me last night."

Smiling, Norman sat back. Though not as intense, he had the same sea-green blue eyes as his son. "Oh? I'm surprised he shared any of that."

That? "Well, he didn't actually. No details. Just mentioned he'd been in a similar position in the past."

Norman studied her a moment. "Once in his business and once in his heart. But they're not my stories to tell." He patted her hand. "Just know that you're welcome here for as long as you want to stay. The Kent family has a long history of being helpers and rescuers. My late wife, Madilyn, could have told you all about it."

Wait, what? "Madilyn? The grill, is it—?"

"Named after my late wife, Noah's mother? Yes, it is. Didn't he tell you that?"

She slowly rose from her chair, grabbing her notebook. "No, he didn't. And I assumed he was the manager, which he said he was…kind of."

"He's that too. He used to be full owner, but that's one of those stories I mentioned is his to tell."

"I see." She set her plate in the sink before passing by the dinette where she paused for a moment.

Norman smiled up at her. "Remember what I said, take time to breathe. You'll get through this. We'll get through this together."

She couldn't do more than nod and scamper off before she burst into tears and blabbed everything. No way could she stay here and continue this charade, deceiving that dear man. Or Noah.

Just her dumb luck, to meet Prince Charming and wind up like one of Cinderella's evil stepsisters.

---

Noah walked the perimeter of the main dining room, adjusting tables, chairs, center arrangements, and service accoutrements until his gut—or like his mother would say, his heart—said everything was in place and ready. He wanted Madilyn's to bring a sense of elegance and comfort to every dining client.

The staff found his routine amusing. One had even described it as superstitious, like those athletes who carry a token or rub a lucky ball before each game. He didn't mind though. Madilyn's was the lady of his life, and he would do whatever needed to keep her happy. Because that's what brought him contentment too.

After nearly losing the place when the pandemic hit, he'd found an angel investor to keep him going—her going. But at a cost. He'd allowed his girlfriend to talk him into letting her father invest in Madilyn's. What started as a silent partnership quickly turned into constant interference, and not just at the business level. Jordan Lancaster had to be in control of everything, including his daughter's life. And the minute that started, Sara bailed on both of them. That's when he learned to never mix business with pleasure, no matter how desperate you might be.

But tonight, Lancaster would do his monthly check on the restaurant to make sure his investment still hummed according to plan. With what Noah had already set aside and the continuing upward trend in profits, he could propose a buyback for the restaurant by the end of the year. And he relished the thought of Madilyn's being all his again.

Voices laughing came from the kitchen, namely one catching his ear. Sheridan had arrived. For three days she'd proven herself a quick learner as well as quick on her feet when necessary. As long as he wasn't in close proximity. And he didn't squelch the chuckle that bubbled up at the thought of it.

"What's so funny?"

He whipped around toward the voice behind him.

With one hand on her hip and the other carrying a notebook, Sheridan gave him an expectant look as she waited for his reply.

"Oh, just lost in my thoughts." He pointed to her notebook. "Have some ideas for me?"

She did a little jump as she brought her notebook up and held it in front of her. "Yes, is now a good time to discuss them?"

He noted her clean shift into professional mode and the confidence she exuded, which only added to her attraction. Plus the excitement that lit her eyes. "Let's sit in a booth." He gestured to the one he usually sat in, doing the books, which gave him a chance to appreciate the front seating area and see the buzz of Pineapple Avenue through the front windows.

Sheridan slid in the same side she did her interview… had it only been a few days? She'd jumped into her schedule with gusto and even cooked dinner for them one evening at the house. His father had again suggested they make the arrangement official, but Noah didn't want to jump into anything too fast. He'd learned his lesson well enough when he mistook his desire to help a girl in college for true love.

Yet helping Sheridan seemed to have helped his father in some way. Perhaps his father needed to feel useful too.

From the portfolio, she pulled out several pages of diagrams mapping out his ideas for the restaurant and connecting them to various social media platforms and live events. "Based upon what you told me as far as your goals for the restaurant, both short and long term, I've mapped out a few ideas that will break down strategies for each quarter of the year."

"Wow, how'd you get all this done in such a short time?"

"I used a productivity app on my phone and printed them out in the office. I hope that's okay?"

"Yeah, of course. I'm just impressed." Very impressed. Techy and savvy. He liked that combo.

Her concerned expression snapped into a pleased smile. "Thank you. Now, if you go this route, you can open up the outdoor and weekly events by the end of the month. You'll see here on this sheet are the names of several local DJs I've vetted and used in the past, and—"

"You planned events before?"

She blinked. "I, uh, yes, I did. I planned a few events as part of my previous position."

"At Serenity Group?"

She hesitated and dropped her gaze. "Yes."

Again, he felt like a heel. Her exuberance seemed to fizzle as soon as he mentioned her previous employer. "It's okay, Sheridan. You don't have to feel bad about any of that. I was just curious, but I won't bring it up again if it upsets you."

"No...no, it's okay. Guess I've gotten used to the scrutiny and judgment that's come with the whole debacle. People tend to think if you worked there that you were in on the scam, which they're still investigating who was fully behind it all."

Why did she sound a little defensive? Was she protecting someone?

"Of course. And I'm sorry you've had to deal with the fallout from that scumbag, Randall Scott." He caught the full effect of his words by the crushed expression on her face. Guess he did it again—spoke his thoughts without thinking about how they might affect someone.

Eyes closed, he took a deep breath and dropped his chin. "Sorry. Just when I think I've dealt with my anger with that whole thing, I find out about someone else who's been hurt by it all. Dad's dealt with it better than I have."

Sheridan blinked moist eyes and cleared her throat. She slid one of the other documents in front of him. "Now, if we go this route, you could optimize on some significant events in the area, like Valentine's Day and St. Patrick's, but I was thinking we could optimize local stuff as well, like rowing competitions and marathons, plus have a presence at the farmer's market downtown. That's a great way to develop more connection to the community at large."

She went into so much detail over the next twenty minutes that he almost forgot how bad he screwed up earlier. And he admired the way she just kept going, not missing a beat.

"This is great work, Sheridan. Let me study it all for a bit and then I'll let you know which direction I want to start implementing." He'd have to run some of this by Lancaster, just to avoid the man's inevitable peevishness over finding out about changes after the fact.

As she gathered her work into a neat stack again, Noah laid his hand on one of hers. "And I'm sorry for losing my cool a bit earlier. Guess I'm still a little upset over the situation."

She nodded and gave him a weak smile. "Trust me, I completely understand."

Acutely aware of the warmth of her skin against his, he squeezed her hand and let go. "I know you do. Which, for some odd reason, makes it worse, I think."

She gabbed her notebook and slid out of the booth, glancing at her watch. "I have a little time before my shift starts. Okay if I run a quick errand?"

"Yeah, sure."

She grabbed her notebook and shot out the front door.

He knew what she was doing—he could spot a runner a mile away. Sheridan still had unresolved issues regarding her former employer. Maybe his father was right about her needing support from others who understood her position, and, right now, that meant him and especially his father. Just as long as Noah didn't mistake that need for something more.

But what if he could help two people with one deal? He turned over one of the sheets of paper she left to make some calculations and came up with an amount he felt Sheridan could afford to rent his guest room.

Tonight he'd present his idea to her after closing hours. And his father would be pleased that his son took his advice, which would make him feel useful. Even though he could hear his mother's voice in his head, telling him to tread carefully, Noah knew this would help Sheridan and his father. He'd draw up a simple monthly contract, that way their arrangement would be official and not just a helping hand, which would give him the separation he needed to keep their arrangement a business transaction and nothing more.

But did he really believe that himself?

# Chapter Seven

Thank goodness she wore her flats today. Sheridan walked as fast as she could without breaking into a full run. What had she gotten herself into? And what were the odds that the one place she lands a job—and even a decent place to live, albeit temporary—turns out to be working for a man who despises her father?

What would Noah think of her if he found out she was Randall Scott's daughter? She couldn't bear the thought of him scrutinizing her like he did her father. She almost lost her cool on that one, but how could she defend her father when she didn't fully believe he was innocent herself?

There...she admitted it to herself. The more she found out, the more she doubted her father's claims of being duped. Even her recent conversations with her mother left her feeling more doubtful than ever. During their last phone call, her mother had mentioned an appointment to consult a divorce attorney. Her heart did a *kathump* again at the thought. Despite being an adult, the idea of her parents divorcing crushed her.

Her mind had turned so far inward that she'd lost awareness of her surroundings and now stood in the middle of the sidewalk, causing others to skirt around her. She needed a distraction. The windows to her left displayed an array of dresses and beachwear, so she darted in, even though she couldn't afford to buy anything. Browsing fashions would help shift her focus and give her mind a break from trying to solve something beyond her control.

However...she didn't realize she's stepped into Sass & Sun until she recognized the changing area. And the sales clerk. She turned around to leave.

"Well, if it isn't Miss Snooty Pants."

Sheridan froze in her tracks and turned around. The woman who had accused her of shoplifting stood with both hands on her hips and her chin lifted, as if prepared for a fight. Sheridan scrambled through her memory for the woman's name. "Kay, right?"

"My friends call me Kay. You can call me Kaleena."

"Sorry." Did she just avoid a confrontation or start a new one? "I'm so sorry for causing you trouble that day. And for my attitude. I have no excuse other than it was a rough day."

Kaleena dropped her arms to her sides and lowered her chin. "I hear ya. We all have days like that. So, what brings you in today? Another rough day?"

The woman actually gave her a sympathetic smile. And seemed friendly.

Confrontation averted.

Sheridan exhaled and slumped her shoulders. "You could say that."

"Is it about your new job?"

"You remembered?"

Kaleena laughed and snorted all at once. "Of course, I

remembered. I know just about everything that goes on around here. So what's got you scramblin' today?"

Noah's face flashed in her mind. She pulled her shoulder back and smiled. "Umm, it's complicated."

Kaleena giggled and pointed at her. "Oh, I see. You're crushing on someone at the job."

"No! I mean, not really." How did the woman read her mail so fast? "He's just been so kind and helpful. Kind of like a knight in shining armor."

"Sounds like a fairy tale."

"That's exactly what I'm afraid of. What happens when the prince discovers he fell for the wicked stepsister instead of the princess?" Sheridan hadn't meant to say so much, but she'd had no one to really talk to through the mess her life had become, and, well, here stood this perfect stranger, ready and willing to listen. Still, she had to keep her guard up.

Kaleena's eyes lit up like fire crackers on the fourth of July. "Now you have to tell me everything."

Sheridan needed a friend...but could she trust Kaleena with her secret? She glanced at her watch. "My shift starts in twenty minutes."

Kaleena dashed to the front, locked the door, and stuck a sign on the door. "Sign says I'll be back in fifteen minutes. Let's go chat in the dressing room area."

She followed Kaleena to the back, sending up a silent prayer for wisdom. Right now she needed an unbiased opinion that even her best friend probably couldn't give her. And Kaleena seemed kind and caring, which brought home for Sheridan again how quick she'd been to judge the woman that day.

Kaleena pulled a chair out from one of the dressing rooms, then patted an olive-green circular ottoman in the center of the space. Mirrors surrounded them. "Come sit and fill me in."

She sank into the plush ottoman and folded her hands on her lap, unsure of what to say first.

Kaleena smiled at her again. "I know we got off to a bad start that day, so let's have a do-over." She held her hand out. "Hi, I'm Kaleena Brooks, owner of this fine establishment."

"Oh! This is your shop!"

"That's right. Been here five years and still going strong." Kaleena did a wiggle in her chair as she brimmed with pride.

She loved this woman's attitude. Smiling, Sheridan shook her hand. "Very impressive, Kaleena. I'm Sheridan Lane. It's a pleasure to meet you."

"Now, share what's on your heart. And I promise that whatever you share stays locked right here." She patted her chest over her heart and made a gesture, imitating turning a key.

For the next fifteen minutes, Sheridan shared her story but kept back certain details. The Scott family had a long-time reputation in Sarasota, and she didn't know how Kaleena felt about recent events. But she could share enough to give her new friend a clear picture of what she was dealing with. Minus the scandal and Noah's connection to it through his father.

"Wow, he really offered you his guest room?"

"Yeah, I know. I'm living in my boss' home. Temporarily, of course." She held her hands out. "And his father lives with him too."

"Noah Kent is a good man." Kaleena nodded her head with a look that said she had more to tell.

"You know him?" Sheridan's caution flags flapped a

little louder. Good thing she hadn't shared the full truth of her situation.

"Yeah, a little bit. Kind of hard not to hear about your neighbor's business when it comes to doing business." She giggled at her pun. "Noah opened the restaurant not too long before I opened this place. He named it after her because she was the one who encouraged him to go after his dream. Too bad she didn't live long enough to see the place really take off. Hardest decision he ever made was bringing in an angel investor, but he couldn't stand the thought of losing the place. It would have been like losing his mother all over again."

"Seems like it worked out okay then."

"You could say that. Except the investor is his ex-girl-friend's father. And you know what they say about doing business with your enemy."

Sheridan cringed inside. "Bad break-up?"

"You could say that. When your father is Jordan Lancaster, it can only end badly."

Sheridan recognized the name and knew the man by reputation in the business world. Jordan Lancaster and his group owned most of the commercial waterfront property in town, which meant they had their hand in most of the well-known and better-known restaurants in town. Her heart went out to Noah at a whole new level.

But that meant Noah and Sara Lancaster were once an item...

She couldn't picture Noah dating someone like that. Or vice versa for that matter. Though she didn't really know Sara, they'd run in some of the same social circles. Sara seemed to always date a certain type—rich and connected.

"Noah broke it off?"

"Nope, she did."

Noah found himself finding reasons to go up front to catch a glimpse of Sheridan. He should wait to have that talk with her, like he planned, but something in him wanted to tell her now, so that she didn't have to worry about finding a place to live anymore. She needed stability in her life right now.

He rubbed the back of his neck as he tried to ignore the blast-from-the-past wise counsel from his mother.

*You can't save everyone, Noah.*

He'd tried to help his college girlfriend, who *fell* hard into the party scene. She'd wound up in the hospital with alcohol poisoning, then moved on to drugs after that. No matter how hard he tried to help her, she couldn't stay clean. And she left a trail of devastating lies in her wake of destruction.

On the verge of failing several of his classes due to her constant need for supervision, he'd finally had to let go. His mother had been right, but it didn't help the gut-wrenching that came when he found out she overdosed a few months later. He'd blamed himself for a long time too.

He'd tried to "help" his ex, Sara too. Only she didn't really want his help either and took it more as interference in getting what she wanted. Which was usually to somehow exasperate her father.

Noah shook off the past and refocused on the here and now. Sheridan seated a large dinner party and headed in his direction to help the server assigned to the table—who was in her last trimester—bring a tray of water glasses to the table. He'd catch Sheridan on the way back and let her know he had a solution for her needing a permanent place to live and he'd fill her in tonight when he got home.

Just as she headed his way, Jordan Lancaster walked in. Thirty minutes early. The man always tried to catch him off guard. His way of controlling the situation.

Including Noah.

When would Jordan finally accept that Sara didn't want to start things back up again? Neither did Noah. If she hadn't broken things off when she did, he would have. They just weren't a good fit.

Noah stepped into Sheridan's path. "I need you to seat Mr. Lancaster at the table I reserved by the wine bar."

Her eyes grew round. "Lancaster?"

"Yes, do you know Jordan?"

"Uh, no, not really. Just heard of him." She darted her eyes to the front waiting area, then jerked her head to face him when Lancaster looked his way and waved. "I'm actually not feeling well. That's why I was coming back here, to grab a sip of soda or something."

"Can you hang on for just a few minutes? You're really great with customers, Sheridan, and I need that with Lancaster right now."

She tilted her head, drawing her shapely brows together in question. "You need my help?"

"Yes, I'll explain later. Along with an idea I have for a more permanent living arrangement for you."

She glanced in Lancaster's direction again and seemed to hesitate. Why did this seem more about Lancaster than her upset stomach? "Okay. I'll try not to puke."

"Or spill anything."

Giving him a cross look, she put her hands on her hips. "Are you sure you want me to seat him?"

A glimmer of hope seemed to creep into her dark eyes as well. What was she hiding?

No time to question her now. "Yes, please. I'll be right

behind you with a special bottle of wine." As she turned to leave, he caught her sleeve. "Use your best customer relations skills."

She bobbed her head in agreement and scooted off toward Lancaster, grabbing a menu as she swept past the greeter podium. Why was she holding the menu in front of her mouth? Was she feeling that bad? He sent a poor man's begging prayer up to heaven, desperate for any help he could get. He signaled the bartender to bring up the bottle he'd selected for Jordan.

When he approached the table, Sheridan whipped around and barreled right into him, shoving the wine bottle against his stomach.

Noah let out an ummph from the gut punch. Moisture seeped into his shirt and splashed his chin.

Sheridan jumped back, arms out and mouth open about ten times the size of her eyes. "I'm so sorry!"

He forced a smile and assessed the bottle. Barely half of a glass had been lost, judging by the stain on his shirt and the level of liquid remaining. But his presentation was shot to hell. And his wardrobe wouldn't be far behind at this rate. "Sheridan, please get me a towel."

Before she could scamper off, the bartender arrived with a bar mop and seltzer. Noah waved off the seltzer for now but took the towel to dry the bottle and his chin.

Jordan stared at him, smirking as he waited for Noah to approach the table. "Did I come at a bad time?"

Noah shook off the man's belittling tone. "Nope, not at all. Still training our new greeter. She gets a little excited about her work sometimes."

"I saw that. Maybe you need someone with more people skills. Sara's considering coming to work for me. She could do a lot for the place, Noah." Lancaster swept his gaze across the room as if he owned it. Which he kind of did, just not all of it.

Part of their agreement was that Noah still called the shots. All of them. He poured a partial glass of wine and set it in front of Lancaster. "I think you'll like this one. Aged in bourbon barrels for several months before bottling. Since you have an affinity for Ports, I thought you might like this one in particular."

Lancaster studied him for a long moment, which meant they weren't done talking about the subject but that he'd go along with Noah—for now. Holding the stem of the glass between his index finger and thumb, Jordan twirled the wine before inserting his nose, then took a sip. He put the glass down and pushed it toward Noah. "Good call."

Noah filled his glass. "Wonderful. I'll send your server over to get you started."

"And then you'll come back to finish our discussion?"

He exhaled and pushed his smile back in place. "I'll be back shortly."

Noah handed the wine bottle off to the bartender on his way to the back to clean up.

It was going to be a long night.

# Chapter Eight

Maybe she should change her last name to Klutz. Or better yet, give the scoop to the newspapers so they can relabel her The Klutzy Diva.

Sheridan hovered near the opening to the main dining room, waiting for Noah to come back. She'd nabbed the seltzer bottle from the bartender and held a fresh bar mop, ready to help Noah clean up.

How had she managed to nearly ruin another expensive bottle of wine? Thankfully Noah had a tight grip—and not just on the bottle but his temper too. She didn't miss that momentary battle that flashed across his face as he fought the urge to yell. And admired him for it. She'd listened to many tirades from her father when marketing campaigns fell short of the goal, even if only by a fraction of a penny on the bottom line.

When he reached the back area, she stepped out from the side hall that led to the employee locker room and back entrance. "Is everything okay with Mr. Lancaster?" She soaked the towel with seltzer and began dabbing his shirt.

Noah held his arms up. "It's fine. I can do that." He made a grab for the towel but caught her wrist too as he tugged it away. The motion pulled her against him.

The normal sea-blue green of his eyes seemed darker, more like stormy waters. Something sizzled in the air between them, but maybe that was Chef searing an order of sea bass. His scent and warmth threatened to overwhelm her senses. She forced herself to step back before she did something she regretted. "Again, I am so sorry."

He poured more seltzer on the towel and wiped at his shirt. "You said you weren't feeling well. Why don't you go home for the night. I can cover the rest of your shift."

She didn't miss the way he didn't look at her. Or maybe he was just distracted with his shirt. Either way, she could tell he didn't want her around. "If you're sure you'll be okay without me."

"I'll be fine. Get some rest. I'll see you later." He did manage a quick smile before he spun around and headed back to the front to greet a guest.

As much as it went against her grain to duck out at a critical time—especially in light of the odd loyalty she felt for a man for whom she'd worked only a week—Lancaster recognizing her would put her back on the street, dealing with scumbag Jimmy and a possible run-in with the stylish homeless dude sporting her fuzzy robe. She rolled her eyes at herself as she yanked her bag out of the locker and swung it over her shoulder.

Besides, if she stayed and Lancaster recognized her, that could only cause more trouble for Noah. Definitely a lose-lose situation. She kept that excuse playing through her head to battle her guilt on the drive home.

Home?

How easily the word came when she thought of her

room in Noah's house. She had an easy rapport with both of the Kent men and found herself wanting to help take care of Norman especially. No doubt where Noah drew his kindness from. And based on the stories his father had shared about Noah's mother, she could understand why he wanted to name the restaurant after her. She'd influenced Noah's passion for the culinary world with her own love of cooking.

But he'd mentioned something about a more permanent living arrangement. Did he find her a place to live? What exactly did he mean by "arrangement"? She kind of liked the one they had. Despite her own family being a bit of a mess, she missed that feeling of belonging.

She parked on the street so Noah could pull into the garage when he arrived home. Once in the door, she intended to go straight to her room, as a sick person would, but she heard some knocking around in the kitchen.

The scene that met her nearly sent her into a fit of laughter if she hadn't caught the frustrated expression on Norman's face. Even still, when she took in the frilly apron he wore and the flour—or was it powdered sugar?—that covered his toes, she giggled. "Are you okay?"

He shook his head before dropping his chin. "Today is Noah's birthday. I wanted to surprise him with the cookies his mother always made for him."

"Oh, I didn't know today was his birthday. He didn't say anything and no one at the restaurant did either." Sheridan grabbed a wad of paper towels, dampened them at the faucet, and then got to work cleaning Norman's feet and the floor.

"I'm not surprised. He hasn't wanted to celebrate it much since her death. Madilyn died the day after his birthday."

No words seemed appropriate. She leaned back on her feet and looked up at Norman with all the compassion she could muster to convey her sympathy. Which wasn't difficult. Her eyes burned with the threat of tears as she ached for these two men.

What a challenging day for Noah…and she'd only made it more difficult.

Her hand stilled when the irony of the situation hit home. Noah had wiped her feet and now, here she crouched, doing the very same for his father. She folded over the damp wad to get a clean side, careful to catch the white dust on his ankles. Once done, she pushed back to her feet. "There. Much better. How about I help you make those cookies?

His instant smile shoved away his previous sadness. "That would be wonderful. Thank you."

"No problem." She put her bag on the floor by the dinette set and made a gesture at the apron he wore. "Have another one of those?"

Norman untied the bow at his back and held it out to her. "No, but you take it. I was only wearing it to remember her."

The thudding ache of her heart stopped her from taking the cherished item. "I'll just use a towel."

He pushed it into her hand with a squeeze. "I'd love to see it on a beautiful woman again."

Sheridan reached for the apron, slow in her reach as she noted the significance of such a beloved item being offered to her, like she'd entered some new inner circle of trust. She slipped the neck loop over her head and then tied the soft fabric behind her back, imagining Madilyn doing the very say thing countless times judging by the state of the fabric. The frilly, yellow edging had come loose on one side and the floral pattern had faded to a dull version of its former vibrancy.

Norman showed her the recipe, a hand-written page in a binder that looked as battered as the apron.

She admired the flourished handwriting on the worn page. The top, right corner had a permanent crease and the bottom half had a stain that puckered the edge. "I used to love to bake as a teenager, but never made shortbread."

He opened the microwave to retrieve a glass bowl filled with liquified butter. "I think I heated it too long."

The edges of the butter had browned and some dripped down the sides.

"No worries. We'll start over." She set the bowl in the sink and prepped another batch.

How could she disentangle herself from a situation she found herself more and more attached to? The Kent men had somehow snagged her heart, and they deserved so much better than what she had to offer. Didn't her life reflect how little she'd appreciated the people who mattered most in her life? Her ex—Jeremy—had accused her of trying to make him into someone he wasn't, just to fit her goals and agenda in life.

And he'd been right. She'd tried to turn him into the man she thought he needed to be only to realize too late that she'd been selfish and self-serving. Nothing like losing the security of her socialite standing and a trust fund to tear her ambitions to shreds.

And now her father seemed a distant memory. Or at least the man she thought she knew. She found herself grieving his loss as if he had died.

While the dough chilled, Sheridan threw together a salad for them and boiled water for pasta. She added olive oil to a sauté pan and added the fresh garlic she found in the fridge, along with an Italian seasoning blend she found in the spice rack.

Once she tossed the cooked pasta with the olive oil mixture, she grated some Parmesan cheese she found in the fridge over the top and set the bowl on the table. Norman had already set the table with placemats that appeared almost as well-loved as the apron and dished out salad into separate bowls.

She served his plate. "It's pretty basic but should taste good."

He took a bite and let out a soft moan. "Delicious. Did your mother teach you to cook like that?"

She paused her fork midway to her mouth. "No, my father actually. He'd make it for me to cheer me up."

Norman wiped his mouth with his napkin and captured her heart with a father-like gaze. "He must be very proud of you, Sheridan."

"I don't know about that." If he had, her father hadn't really expressed it. That had never been his style.

"Trust me, parents never stop being proud of their kids, no matter what."

She chewed a bite of pasta as she digested his words. "Noah's very lucky to have a father like you."

"I guess. I'm sure he never expected to have his father living with him at this point in time. Just when it seemed like he and I would be okay, I wind up broke and have to move in with him."

The sick stomach she feigned at the restaurant became a sudden reality. She set her fork down and launched to her feet before he could see her building tears. "Time to preheat the oven and check the cookie dough."

Thankful for the continued distraction, she sliced the dough into quarter-inch thick slices and lined them on the cookie sheet. A glance at the recipe reminded her of the next steps before slipping the sheet into the oven.

She'd make sure to retire to her room and turn out the lights as soon as the cookies were done and the kitchen cleaned. No way could she face Noah tonight because the guilt-laden brick in her throat would force her to barf up the truth. His idea about her living arrangements would have to wait until morning. She'd beg Emma for the use of her couch and compose herself so she could walk away from two of the kindest men she'd ever met before she did any more harm.

The timer dinged. She opened the oven. Heat wafted up around her face and neck as she noted the hint of gold near the edges of the cookies. She pulled the baking sheet out, then closed the door. The aroma of baked butter and sugar made her mouth water.

She turned to show the cookies to Norman but froze in place when saw Noah standing in the doorway to the kitchen with a frown on his face.

"What do you think you're doing?"

She bounced her gaze to the cookie sheet. "Baking—"

"I thought you said you were sick?" He took a step into the kitchen.

Norman rose from the table and held his hand out in front of Noah to stop him. "She's helping me bake your favorite cookies for your birthday."

Noah stared at the cookies before tilting his head. "Is that mom's apron?"

Not at all what she expected to happen. She nearly dropped the cookie sheet onto the counter in her rush to get her hands free to take the apron off. "Sorry. Was just trying to help."

After laying the apron on a clean part of the counter,

she dashed past both of the Kent men and made a beeline for her room. She'd lock the door and hide under the covers.

And call Emma for a bailout.

---

His father still hadn't stopped frowning at him. "I think you hurt her feelings."

"I don't like being lied to, Dad. You should know that better than anyone since you're the one that taught me that." The aroma of shortbread still had him tripping over the memories of his mother. Add to that his run-in with Lancaster, who had made his point clear by the end of the evening—find a position for Sara and make it a good one. Nothing less than a managerial position. Or he'd make his investment a loan with a due date of yesterday.

Noah had breathed a sigh of relief when Lancaster finally left. Once the place was closed and mostly clean, he'd sent everyone home with a plan to come in early tomorrow to finish the job. Why? So he could bring Sheridan some soup from the chef because she was sick.

But she didn't appear sick. Had she lied?

He held up the bag. "She said she wasn't feeling well so I brought her some soup."

His father pointed to her partially eaten dinner. "She never said anything about not feeling well. When she got home and found me making a mess in the kitchen, she jumped in to help."

He checked out the cookies laid out on the baking sheet in neat little rows. He picked one up and took a bite, closing his eyes as the shortbread melted in his mouth. Just like he remembered.

"Happy birthday, Son."

Noah opened his eyes.

His father stood in front of him and gave him a hug. "I think there's a young woman in the house that's in need of soup."

Noah nodded. After he popped the last bite of cookie into his mouth, he slid the soup container out of the bag and headed to her side of the house. The light under the door went out. He paused. Maybe he should leave her alone. Apologize in the morning. He turned around to go back into the kitchen.

But he really wanted to tell her his idea about making her room rental official. He spun around and barreled right into her.

Sheridan fell back onto the floor, landing on her backside as the container of soup flew from his hand, arced into the air, and landed on the floor in front of her with a *splat*. The smell of chicken broth filled the air and chunks of chicken and carrots covered the tile and Sheridan.

She held her hands out, shaking noodles from her fingers. Broth dripped from her face and eyelashes.

"I'm sorry." They both said it at the same time.

Noah dashed into the kitchen and grabbed a roll of paper towels. He crouched in front of her and handed her a wad of paper towels while he sopped up broth from the floor. A rogue noodle hung from her hair.

He helped her up. "There's a noodle in your hair. May I?"

She tucked her chin. "Please."

He used just the tips of his thumb and forefinger so as not to smush the noodle into her hair. "You know, we really need to stop running into each other like this."

When she didn't laugh, he dropped his gaze to her face.

She stared up at him, eyes red as if she'd been crying. "I'm really, really sorry."

Her voice barely made the whisper zone. Seeing her distress tore at something deep in him. He wanted to rescue her from the constant shadow that seemed to follow her around and make things better. She deserved that, deserved to be appreciated...cared for.

He lowered his head. "Don't be. This one's on me." Unable to resist the softness of her lips and the sadness in her eyes, he ran his thumb down the smooth line of her jaw and cupped her cheek.

She tilted her mouth up to meet his as he captured her lips in a gentle, lingering kiss.

Just as soft as he'd imagined, yet firm in her return. She leaned into him. Her soft moan sparked his desire.

He deepened the kiss, pulling her tighter against him.

The taste of chicken broth mixed with the lingering aroma of shortbread sent a wake-up call to his brain. Sheridan worked for him and he was about to offer her the option of leasing his guest room to help her out. Getting romantically involved could easily be interpreted as him taking advantage of her. And he could never do that to her, or anyone.

Besides, he had enough to deal with now that Lancaster had turned the oven to broil—a great reminder of what happened last time he mixed business with romance.

He stepped back. "I'm thinking this is probably a bad idea."

She blinked, then nodded. "Probably." Her chin trembled.

He took her hand. "I'm sorry. I don't want to complicate things for either of us. But I do have an idea that I think you'll like."

Her eyes widened with what looked like hope.

"Rental prices are through the roof with the tourist season, so if you're interested in staying, you can rent my guest room. We can even make it official with a lease. You've already been a big help to my dad so we'll make that part of the cost, you pitching in around the place."

Tears welled up in her eyes. "That's so generous of you. I, uh...I—"

He held his hands up, palms out. "And no strings attached. I want to be clear about that." He wagged his finger between them. "I promise I won't let that happen again."

Her expression shifted for a quick moment to either doubt or disappointment. He couldn't tell. But then she sighed and gave him a small smile. "Okay. I'll stay."

# Chapter Nine

Sheridan parked in the back parking lot and then walked over to Pineapple Avenue to meet Emma at Java Joes. As she turned the corner to the main sidewalk, she spotted her friend sitting at an outside table. Two cups of coffee sat on the table, along with a plate in the middle with a muffin.

Emma stood when she recognized Sheridan and gave her a hug before leaning back to look Sheridan straight in the face. "How are you? And I mean honestly."

She never could hide her feelings from Emma. Guess that's what made her a best friend and at the moment, her only friend, really. "I'm...surviving."

Emma pointed to the opposite chair. "Sit. Fill me in. I'm sorry I wasn't more helpful the last two weeks. My parents decided to stay an extra week, but couldn't find anything on the beach so they decided to just stay with me longer." She rolled her eyes.

"They survived another week on your pull-out?" Sheridan had spent the night on occasion on Emma's couch and learned early on to leave the thing closed up if she wanted to get any sleep.

"Barely. Dad went to see his chiropractor his first day back." Emma covered her mouth as she giggled.

Sheridan sat back in her chair, laughing with her. A layer of stress sloughed off. She took a sip of her coffee. "Just the way I like it."

"I know. I remember. You haven't changed your coffee order since college."

As she thought back to their days as roommates, she smiled. "I miss that."

Emma leaned forward. "My place doesn't have near enough closet space, but you're welcome to bunk on my couch for however long you need it."

"It's okay. I think I found a place."

"Think?" Emma squinted one eye at her as she turned her head to the side.

"Yeah, my boss offered to rent his guest room to me. You know, make it official."

Emma's expression turned deadpan. "How much and what's the catch?"

She giggled. "Cheap and no catch. Just help out around the place."

Emma raised her brows. "Help out how?"

When had her friend become so suspicious? "Will you stop it? Noah made it clear that's not going to happen. Besides, his father lives there too."

Emma nearly choked on her bite of muffin. "His father?" She coughed and took a swig of her coffee. "That might be worse."

"Oh stop. Norman is a sweet man who happens to be down on his luck." She glanced away, hoping to hide her thoughts. "Just like me."

Her friend narrowed her eyes to catlike slits, which really did make her look rather feline, with her startling blue eyes and reddish-blonde hair. "What are you hiding?"

Sheridan slumped in her chair and sighed. "His father lives with him because he invested his retirement savings with Serenity Group."

"And lost everything..." Emma put her coffee down and leaned forward. "Do they know—"

She shook her head.

"Oh, Sheri, what are you going to do? You can't stay there. What's going to happen when they find out?"

She held her hands up. "I'll just have to make sure they don't until I can figure out the best time to tell them."

Emma spun her head back and forth, checking to make sure no one could hear them, then leaned forward. "That, my dear, is a disaster waiting to happen. But I love you and my couch will be there when the bottom falls out of your bed."

Noah walked out of the bank a resigned man. His buddy Eric couldn't find a way to qualify him for a loan to buy out Lancaster's investment, so that left him with one choice.

He'd have to hire Sara at the restaurant. All he could do is hope she had a different path in mind and refused. Her father had a bad habit of trying to control her life, which drove her batty. So anytime Noah had made a suggestion or tried to help her while they were dating, she'd interpreted it as him trying to control her too. That's what she accused him of when she broke things off.

Maybe she'd see his offer as another attempt to 'control

her' and turn him down. Then he'd be off the hook until Lancaster came up with some other scheme. In the meantime, he'd either have to find another angel investor or hope and pray his plans to increase business paid off. In a big way...

Noah took his time walking back to the restaurant, taking in the sights on Main Street. The morning had crept into early afternoon already and many of the local joints buzzed with their lunch crowd. With the addition of lunch seating for Madilyn's, he'd have to hire additional staff and almost double their food orders. But if the profit margin increased beyond expenses, thereby allowing him to buy out Lancaster, then Noah would do the extra work needed to make it happen.

He wanted to pick Sheridan's brain for more ideas too. So far her suggestions were spot on and her strategies refreshing. She knew how to think outside of the box, and he appreciated that more than anything.

Well, almost anything. He still couldn't stop thinking about their kiss.

He slid into the booth where he usually sat before opening hours to look over the numbers and Sheridan's latest suggestions. Since they made her stay at Casa Kent official, she'd remained distant and polite, quick to do her part around the house but also quick to retreat to her room. He didn't like that at all, but he kept reminding himself— especially when his thoughts wandered to that kiss—that it was probably for the best.

And yet his mind loved to revisit that place and try to recapture the feel of her lips and body against his. Everything about that moment—about her—felt right. Didn't help that the soup of the day was chicken noodle. Chef Margot's special recipe would now forever bring him back to that moment, the way she felt when he pulled her closer—

The front door whooshed open and in walked Sara Lancaster. The lingering images of Sheridan faded as he checked his watch. Thirty minutes early. Sara had picked up on her father's disarmament tactics, but Noah had prepared and suspected as much. He knew this meeting would either entail him telling her he had bought her father out or offering her a position as assistant manager. Faced with the latter, his hopes rested on her turning him down.

Noah slid out of the booth and rose to his full height to greet her. "Sara, it's good to see you again."

"Noah." She drew out the first syllable of his name and finished the second through her nasal cavity.

The sound made him want to cringe. Probably something she picked up from some recent movie or music star she chose to mimic. He held his hand out to the opposite seat in the booth. "Please, sit."

Sara slid in across from him, her chin slightly lifted as she stared at him.

"So, Jordan tells me you want to get to know the restaurant business."

"That's right." She nodded, her expression serious.

"And that you want a job here."

"Yes." She nodded and gave him a confident smile.

She would have told him to take his job and shove it somewhere unpleasant by now if this was only her father's idea. That meant she wanted Noah to hire her and expected that he would *because* of her father.

Time for another tactic. He sat back in his seat, using the moment to formulate a direct approach. "So, Sara, why the sudden interest in the food industry? You didn't want anything to do with the place when we were together and your father first invested. I assumed this was your father's idea."

"It was…at first, but then I started thinking about it and realized it made sense."

"Oh?" He leaned forward.

"This is the one area my father isn't *directly* involved in."

He nodded. "I see. You want to work, just not directly under your father."

"Exactly." She finally smiled. "I want something of my own."

Warning bells went off in his head. "Let me be clear, Sara. Madilyn's is my restaurant. Your father is just an investor."

"For now."

Was that a threat? His gut surged upward and his chest muscles tightened. "What does that mean?"

She shrugged and gave him a coy look. "You never know what the future holds, Noah. I'm all about keeping my options open."

Her expression turned deadpan again, but she had that tell-tale glint in her eye, which usually meant she had a scheme in mind that would not benefit him. He struggled to remember what exactly had attracted him to her in the first place.

This side of their break-up gave him the perspective to see that he'd matured more than he realized and wanted more out of life. He wanted a partner—one he chose out of wisdom and not out of desperation. Or pressure. Or… convenience, which Sara most definitely had been, if he were to be honest with himself.

He had to find a way out of this mess. "All right then,

the only position I can offer you is assistant manager. You'll shadow me until you learn the ropes. We're planning to add a lunch seating—just a few days at first—to test the waters."

"Then once I'm trained you'll make me a full manager of the lunch shift." Her tone started out as a question but ended as a statement bordering on a command.

Not on your life. "We'll see how you do first." He pushed over the standard hiring forms for her to fill out.

She made a face. "Really?"

"Everyone has to fill these out."

She went to town on the paperwork, filling out the blanks with her oversized handwriting, much like he remembered how the girls in high school would write on the notes they slipped to each other in class.

"I'll be right back."

"Sure thing. Boss." She gave him a mock salute.

The dread in his gut slurped and boiled, like a stew left on the stove too long. As he headed to the back of the restaurant, Sheridan appeared at the kitchen entrance, dressed in a stylish pink dress and black heels.

"Hey there. Ready to look over the event plans for next month?" She grinned as if excited about the prospect.

He liked how she bumped her attire up for the Friday and Saturday evening crowd. Somehow she knew to do that without being asked. Sheridan would make a better assistant manager at this point than Sara would.

"Sure, just as soon as I'm done with a new hire." He pointed a thumb over his shoulder. "Sara Lancaster will be our new assistant manager, once I get her trained."

Sheridan leaned to the side to look at Sara. Her smile fell faster than the wine bottle she knocked out of his hands that first day. "I, uh…I see."

"Don't worry. I'll make sure she's totally up to speed with how we do things around here. Otherwise, we'll have to," he paused, trying to find the words to delicately say he'd find a way to get rid of her, "rethink her position."

# Chapter Ten

Why did the universe seem out to get her these days?

Sheridan hovered near the locker room, waiting for Sara Lancaster's arrival for her first day as assistant manager. They didn't really know each other, but what if Sara recognized her? Sheridan crossed her arms in front of her and held one hand over her heart, feeling the rapid beat against her palm. While the rest of the restaurant hummed to the usual rhythm of mid-afternoon preparations, her pulse pounded like a rap song on speed.

Didn't help that she'd tossed and turned most of the night in anticipation of a potential crash and burn today, and had consumed multiple cups of coffee to compensate.

"You okay?"

At the sounds of Noah's voice, She whipped around and forced a smile. "Yes, why?"

He frowned at her. "You look really pale. You sure you're over that bug you had?"

"I'm fine. Really."

The front door opened and in walked Sara, dressed in a

clingy jumpsuit covered in a red and orange hibiscus print. Red pumps finished the ensemble, which made Sheridan miss her Jimmy Choo heels.

She dropped her arms. "I'll go wait in your office until you're finished."

"Sure." He didn't even look at her. Did he still have feelings for Sara? The idea made her want to dump the soup of the day over her head, but that would be a waste of really good seafood gumbo.

She made a dash for his office. Somehow she had to avoid Sara as much as possible. And hope her father didn't come in to check on her. She'd attended several business luncheons with her own father over the last several years and had met Jordan Lancaster at several of them. The man never forgot a name.

Sheridan busied herself with pulling out the diagram she'd made, mapping out her ideas for next month's events and how to promote each one. She used four magnets to attach it to Noah's whiteboard, careful not to mess up the schedule he had laid out showing shifts and deliveries.

His voice came from the hallway. "Let me give you a copy of our employee guidelines."

Sara followed him in. "Guidelines? I didn't realize you were so formal here?"

"We all need to be on the same page to keep things running smoothly."

Sheridan jerked around to face the board. What could she do to look busy? She glanced down, grabbed one of the dry erase markers, and started making a list of the social media platforms the restaurant had a presence on.

"Sheridan, this is Sara Lancaster."

She did a quick glance over her shoulder and kept her voice bubbly. "Hi there."

Noah moved into her peripheral vision. "Sheridan is a greeter by night and my marketing guru by day."

His marketing guru? Warmth spread through her chest at hearing his praise, but she continued writing as she faced the board. "Just doing my part to make Madilyn's the best place in town."

"Is Sheridan part of your team planning the promotions for the new lunch hours?"

Sheridan paused her writing and shot her gaze to Noah.

"Yes, actually, she will be." Noah's grin widened as he looked at her.

Sara's voice seemed closer this time. "Great, then I guess that means we'll be working together a fair bit, Sheridan. Why don't you fill me in on what you're doing there on the board."

Might as well get it over with. She put the top on the marker and turned around.

Sara stood with her hand out, waiting...but said nothing.

Could it be the universe had shifted in her favor? Not that she put much stock in things like that but sometimes...

"Sheridan?" Noah sent a concerned look at her.

"Ah, right, sorry about that. Just trying to figure out where to start." With a silent sigh of relief, she shook Sara's hand before turning back to the whiteboard to begin explaining her plan.

Maybe the universe liked her after all.

---

Despite Sheridan appearing somewhat unsettled at first, the thirty minutes spent discussing future events and the soon-to-start lunch seating went smoother than he anticipated.

Perhaps there was a blessing in disguise in Lancaster's pushiness. Sara seemed motivated, which should make him less unsettled over having her there, but for some reason, sent his suspicions up a notch. He'd never known her to operate without an agenda.

And seeing Sheridan in action brought back his earlier reflection of her making an excellent assistant manager. She learned fast and had great business instincts. And as an assistant manager, she'd work more closely with him. He liked that idea entirely too much and mentally filed it under the label 'too hot to touch.'

Sara sauntered off to the kitchen with Manny to learn more about how the kitchen worked while Sheridan gathered the ad mock-ups she'd created from his desk. She hadn't said a word since Sara left.

He moved close enough to where she stood by the whiteboard to catch the scent of flowery perfume. Reminded him of the gardenia bushes his father had planted for his mother. "Those look great, by the way. Thank you for putting so much work into this."

"Happy to. Madilyn's is a great restaurant." She moved one of the magnets off the diagram she'd put up.

"No, leave it up."

She lowered her arms. "Won't it be in the way of your schedule?"

"No, it needs to be *part* of the schedule."

She nodded and put the magnet back.

He pointed to the part of her diagram that mapped out a Sunday brunch seating. He'd thought about that possibility once they had a handle on the lunch seating, but he didn't recall mentioning it to her yet. "How did you know I wanted to add a Sunday brunch?"

"I didn't. I wanted to suggest it though. But something

unique, like that place that has a live gospel band. Blue Rooster, or something like that."

"Yeah, I know the place. And I agree, something unique to Madilyn's." He took a step closer to her. He'd always wanted a partner in this business, someone who shared his passion and excitement for growing it into more than just a place to eat.

"Just makes sense." Her smile faltered. "But I didn't want to overstep."

He chuckled. "If that's what you call overstepping, then do it more often."

"Really?" She scrunched her face into that cute smile she did when she doubted herself.

"Yeah, you have great instincts, Sheridan." The need to be closer to her overwhelmed him. She had to feel the pull between them. Just a couple steps and he'd be close enough to touch those silky strands of hair she always pulled down around her face when she wore it up. "In fact, if you're willing to stick around a while, I'd like to see if we could make your position more official on the marketing management side and relieve you of your greeting responsibilities."

Her eyes widened. "Wow, I'd love that."

He knew he should resist, especially in light of what he just offered her. He still believed mixing business with pleasure was like putting an egg on a counter without something to hold it in place. Take your eyes off of it and you'll have a mess on the floor. But with Sheridan, he wanted to find out if things could be different, if he could work with and date her too.

Was it worth the risk? If things didn't work out, he could lose her completely.

Right now he wanted to kiss her more than ever, but would she think that was part of the deal? And the way she kept looking at him, as if she wanted it as much as he did, crumbled his resolve to resist. He reached out and linked his fingers in hers.

"Hey boss, shipment just arrived."

Noah jerked his hand to his waist and rubbed the back of his neck with the other one. "I'll be right there, Manny."

Providential interruption? Maybe the big guy upstairs was trying to protect him.

One hand on the doorjamb, Manny leaned into the doorway, then noted Sheridan's presence. "Hey, Sheridan."

"Hi, Manny." Sheridan grabbed her folio. "My shift is about to start."

Manny ducked out as Sheridan followed him.

He didn't like the way things felt so...unfinished. "Sheridan."

As she spun around outside the door, the lighting in the hallway cast a soft glow over her hair and shoulders, enhancing her beauty. "Yeah?"

He cleared his throat to find his voice again. "Think about what we talked about. Since it's a new position, I'd like to hear what you think it should look like."

She smiled and nodded. "Will do."

# Chapter Eleven

Now that her shift was over, Sheridan sat in her little car in the parking lot, unsure of what she should do. She needed to talk to someone.

After what she felt today in Noah's office, neither one of them could deny the attraction growing between them. She almost felt guilty for his attraction to her. Once he found out who she really was, he'd hate her—and himself—for falling for her. No, she couldn't let that happen.

Maybe instead of accepting this new position, she should just find another job and save him and his father from the grief she would ultimately bring to their lives. If it had been any other time in her life, she wouldn't have cared. But she couldn't do that to Noah. He was too...good. So caring.

She glanced at her phone—almost ten. Emma said she had a date tonight and probably wouldn't be home for another hour at least. She prayed Emma had a good time but didn't fall too fast for this new guy, which she had a tendency to do, which then scared the guy off before he had a chance to decide if he liked her fan-girl style devotion.

As Sheridan was about to give up and go home, Kaleena came out of the back door to her shop, balancing a stack of clothing that eclipsed her head and threatened to topple.

Sheridan jumped out of her car and jogged on the front of her heeled shoes to catch the cascade of fabric. But too late. Several garments fell and puddled on the ground.

"Oh shoot!" Kaleena grunted as she shifted the remaining stack to see the ground.

Sheridan crouched to snatch the hangers up. "Does the five-second rule apply to clothing too?"

Kaleena snorted. "I won't tell if you won't. Can't be any worse than some of the people who come in from the beach to try things on."

"Ew...seriously?"

"Oh, the stories I could tell. I had to throw a silk shirt away because even the cleaners couldn't get the smell of suntan lotion out of it."

"Wow." She followed Kaleena to her car. "So, what's the deal? If I didn't know you owned the shop, I'd be concerned about being an accessory to a crime."

Kaleena let out a belly laugh. "Nothing worth going to jail for in this batch. They're discontinued items that have run the course on the sale rack. About once a year I donate a rack to the Exchange."

"I don't think I've heard of this place."

"I don't expect you would have, Miss Snooty Pants." She winked at Sheridan.

"Hey now, I've amended my snobbery." Though she did still feel a tad embarrassed when she thought back to that day.

"I'm just teasing. You and I are just fine. But you should check out this place. They don't just sell clothing but furniture and household items too. All used and the profits go to battered women and help fund scholarships to help promote education."

"Wow, sounds like a great place." Sheridan liked the idea of used items getting a second chance instead of adding to the landfill. Everything—and everyone—deserved a second chance, right?

Maybe even her father...his case would conclude tomorrow and for some reason he wanted Sheridan to come early so he could speak to her but he wouldn't tell her why. She didn't have a clue what to expect and that made her more apprehensive than anytime she could recall.

"That's where I'm headed in the morning with this bunch." Kaleena laid her stack in the back of her oversized SUV.

After a quick brush off and examination, Sheridan added the clothes she rescued. "I think they're fine."

"Great. Thank you." She closed the hatch. "So, what brings you my way besides coming to my rescue."

"Oh, nothing. Just saw you needed help." Sheridan glanced down. Her jog to help Kaleena left a scratch on the toe of her left shoe, something she would have fussed over in the past, but tonight, she didn't care. Helping Kaleena was worth it.

"Come on, now. Something's weighing on you." She moved closer, looking rather conspiratorial. "Is something brewing with that gorgeous boss of yours?"

She let out a soft laugh. "No, not really..."

How did Kaleena manage to frown and raise a brow all at once to convey her disbelief without saying a word?

"Okay, yes, something along those lines." She paused to

consider how much to share. "Basically, Noah wants me to create my own position at the restaurant. He likes my ideas and wants my focus to be on growing and promoting Madilyn's presence in town."

Kaleena's eyes widened to match the circle of her mouth. She swatted Sheridan's arm. "That's so great! You should go for it."

"I'd love to, but…it's getting more complicated. We, uh…kissed."

Kaleena clapped her hands together in rapid succession. "Oooooooh! I knew it! I knew something had changed."

"How did you know!?" Sheridan tried to keep her voice down but Kaleena's excitement was too contagious.

"I ran into Noah at the coffee shop yesterday. The man had a pep to his step and a mile to his smile. Let me tell you." She giggled and did a little wiggle with her hips. "Mmm, this is so gooooood."

Sheridan couldn't resist laughing with her new friend. She wished she could just tell Kaleena the whole story— even that felt deceitful to some degree. But she didn't want to risk losing the one other friend she had in the world at the moment. "I wish I could share your optimism, Kaleena. Honestly, I think I'm in over my head."

She put her hands on her hips. "Then you're overthinking it, Sheri. Who says you have to make a decision right this minute? Give things a little more time. The answer will present itself."

Sheridan's eyes burned, making her blink. Somehow Kaleena had picked up on Sheridan's nickname without even hearing it from someone else. Only Emma ever called her that. And her father. She felt her attachment to this woman growing more and more, which made hiding the truth even worse.

She had to find a way to tell her—and Noah—and Norman!—the truth about who she was. But would they believe that she had nothing to do with her father's 'supposed' embezzlement? Just about all of her friends in the social scene had dropped her like a hot tater tot.

She hugged Kaleena good night and went back to her car to head home. Sheridan found herself caring more and more about Noah, Norman, and Kaleena. Especially Noah…somehow she'd resist if he showed up at her bedroom door.

Her stomach twisted into a knot tighter than the cinnamon bun she had for lunch. How much longer could she keep this charade going? If the truth didn't destroy her, the growing guilt would. She didn't see how she could start a relationship with him without first confessing the truth.

But what if Noah hated her and asked her to leave his house and Madilyn's? The thought of detangling herself from their little family made her heart hurt in the worst way.

---

Surprised that he'd made it home before Sheridan, Noah lingered in the kitchen preparing the ingredients to make omelets for them both. Though it was late, he was starving and she had to be too. He wanted to talk to her—more than that if he was going to be honest. He wanted to finish what they'd almost started in his office earlier that day. He wanted Sheridan Lane in his life in the worst way. But he had to be sure he wasn't mistaking his need to rescue her as something deeper. At this point, he had no doubt that he could fall for her. Hard.

Like the procedures they had at the kitchen, he'd set in

place boundaries to protect himself, but right now his psyche was setting off alarms of impending fire. He'd used caution thus far, but part of him wanted to jump in and start something with Sheridan. But would he get burned?

The faint sound of an engine in the driveway and then her key in the door signaled her arrival. The skillet sizzled as he poured in the egg mixture.

Her heels clicked on the tile. "You're still up."

"And starving. How about you?" He tossed a glance over his shoulder along with the kitchen towel he used to wipe his hands.

"Very much. Didn't have time to eat today."

"Then have a seat. Omelet on the way."

"Do I have time to change?"

The temptation to say a cheesy line like *don't ever change* hit him, but he resisted. She looked amazing already in the pinstripe slacks and red button-down silk top she wore today. "If you're quick."

"You won't even realize I left." She dashed out of the kitchen, oversized bag in tow.

These days he always felt her lack of presence. And that was part of what scared him a little. How had he slipped this deep so fast?

She returned just as he plated her omelet and added some finely chopped green onion to garnish the top.

He set the plate in front of her at the table.

Hair piled on her head now, she looked rather cozy in a pair of yoga pants and a pale pink, oversized T-shirt. Not her otter shirt this time. This one said *little boss lady*.

If she only knew…

"Where's Norman?"

"He went to bed early. Said he wore himself out working in the yard."

"I'm not surprised. He's determined to get that flower bed weeded out." She took a bite and made a yummy sound that made him want to reach across the table and hold the fork for her.

"I know. He wants to plant a butterfly garden so he can paint it."

She put her fork down. "Tell me about your mother."

Intrigued, he put his fork down and wiped his mouth. "What do you want to know?"

"What was she like?"

He sat back, thinking about where to begin or what to share. "Independent, bold, loved without limitations, and regretted not having more children."

She let out a soft laugh. "Wow, I'm impressed. Most people can't even sum up themselves in so few words."

"She was also a psychologist who specialized in family therapy."

"And now I understand." She did this adorable little tilt and dip with her head. Something she usually did when she had a brilliant idea or new understanding about something.

His turn to laugh. "What does that mean?"

After finishing her last bite, she pushed her plate away. "You're clear-minded and directed, yet compassionate and forthright. Your mother did a great job teaching you to be self-aware without being self-absorbed." She dropped her gaze. "I wish my parents had done that for me."

"Tell me about them." He stacked his plate on hers and carried them to the sink.

"Not much to tell really. Just had to learn some difficult things later in life." Voice subdued, she stared at her hands on the table. The sadness he'd seen peeking out on occasion came back. What difficult things had she experienced that would keep that shadow lurking in her life?

She pushed up from the table. "Speaking of parents, I better get to bed. I told my dad I'd meet with him in the morning. Bright and early."

"Coffee date?"

"Something like that." She started to leave the kitchen.

In three long strides, Noah caught up with her. "I'll walk you to your door."

She paused, studying him. "Wow, first he makes me dinner and now he's walking me to my door. Such a gentleman."

"Ah, well, just trying to be selfless." Didn't take them long to reach her bedroom door.

She turned to face him. "Thank you for a lovely evening."

He brushed away a piece of hair that had caught on her eyelash. "Glad it wasn't a noodle this time."

"Me too."

"And no mess."

"You caught me on a good day." Her gaze dropped to his mouth, drawing him in even closer.

"Caught you? Is that what I've done?" He ran the side of his forefinger up to her chin and nudged it up.

Her eyes darted back and forth, drowning him in their deep depths. "I believe so."

Light at first, he brushed his lips against hers, keen to catalog and remember every aspect of her. But like a chemical reaction, heat burst between them. He pulled her closer and deepened the kiss. When she slid her hands around to his back to hold onto him, he slid his hand to her head and twined his fingers into her silky hair.

He didn't know how long they kissed—could have been ten seconds or ten minutes. But he sensed she didn't want to take things further yet and neither did he. Not yet.

He lifted his head and almost recaptured her lips for another kiss at the way her eyes, filled with longing, captured his heart. "I'm seriously falling for you, Sheridan, but I don't want to rush this."

She blinked and nodded. "I need to tell you…"

He rubbed his thumbs across her cheeks. "Tell me what?"

"I…uh…I feel the same about you." The shadow returned, and she seemed to retreat.

Whatever she battled, he'd find a way to help her. He kissed her one last time. "Good night, Sheridan."

"Good night, Noah."

He let go of the breath he held as she went into her room and shut the door.

Good thing she didn't stop and look back or he might have followed her in.

# Chapter Twelve

Why hadn't she just told him the truth?

Sheridan asked herself that question most of the night after their impromptu date. That's what it had felt like, the way he made her dinner and then walked her to her door. She kept replaying their kiss through her mind like a giddy teenager. And his confession about how he was falling for her

Would he still fall for her when he found out she'd lied about who she was? She should have told him when she mentioned meeting her father. Would have been an ideal time, but he was being so sweet and kind, making her dinner and asking about her life. She wanted so much to tell him more, but she'd chickened out. And she left this morning before he came out of his room already in a rush to make it to the courthouse on time.

She had to tell him tonight. Before he found out some other way. And before whatever this was budding between them had a chance to fully bloom. Or explode? She shook away her thoughts and focused on where she needed to go.

The courthouse teemed with people and reporters. She figured the easiest way not to get noticed would be to walk into the courthouse as if she were an average Jane called to jury duty. She matched her pace to a rather large man walking in front of her, kept her cool, and in she strode in as if she had someplace to be.

Which she did.

At security, she made sure she smiled and blended in. The two reporters standing on the opposite side didn't even notice her. Once she collected her bag, she found her way to the room where her father said he would be waiting.

She knocked first.

The door opened a sliver, revealing her father's lawyer. "Sheridan, good to see you." He opened the door to admit her and then closed it behind her.

Her father sat at a small conference table, dressed in his usual three-piece suit, and looked as regal as ever. She'd noticed a weariness about him when she saw him last, but this time he looked downright exhausted.

He rose to hug her and then kissed her cheek—something he rarely did unless it was serious. "Good to see you, Sheri."

"Hi, Daddy." She took a seat next to where he sat. "Are you okay? You look tired."

He gave her a weak smile. "I am tired and ready for this to be over."

She patted his hand. "Today's the last day, right? You'll be free in no time." She managed a smile, determined to stay positive for him.

Her father glanced at his lawyer before looking back at her. "Sheri...I've decided to change my plea."

A nervous laugh bubbled up before she could stop it.

She didn't like the sound of that at all. "Why? What are you saying?"

He covered her hand with his other one. "There's no getting out of this, Sheri. If I plead guilty, they'll make me a deal. One I'd be a fool to refuse."

She sought a reaction from his lawyer, but he seemed more interested in the papers in front of him. Or was he pretending to be busy? "But you didn't do it. That's what you said…"

"I know. Because I couldn't stand the thought of you thinking ill of me. But it's time to tell the truth."

Trying to absorb what he said, she pulled her hand away and sat back in her chair. "Why? You already had so much money. Why did you do that to all those people?"

His eyes turned watery, something she hadn't seen since her grandmother died. "I made some bad investments and we were about to go bankrupt. I had to do something."

"Oh, Daddy." Her eyes filled with tears. She witnessed firsthand what had happened to one of her father's victims. And Norman was right—she'd suffered as well. Lost her home and way of life. But what could she do? He was still her father. Hadn't she made a string of bad decisions in her life too?

But he'd lied to her.

And she had lied too. Still was to Noah. And to Norman. If she threw a stone, her own glass house would shatter along with her father's.

Or already had.

She sighed. "I've done some things in my life that I wish I could take back. But they were mostly to my detriment, not others. I really wish you'd just told us what was going on. We would have figured out what to do together."

"I know. I'm sorry." He seemed quite remorseful, but was that only in light of what he faced next?

She swallowed, hesitated, but she had to understand, just a little bit at least. Maybe if she'd never met Noah and Norman, it wouldn't matter as much, but she had and carried a burden now for someone her father's actions had hurt. "Did you ever stop and think through what could happen to all those people who lost their savings? What it could mean to their lives?"

"I thought I could replace it. I thought I had more time." He looked so broken and weak.

She couldn't bear to make him any more upset, but she had to say one more thing. "I wanted so much to believe you were innocent, Daddy. I just couldn't imagine you doing something that would ruin other people's lives. Including my own. And mother's."

"I'm so sorry, Sheri. I wish I could go back and fix everything."

His lawyer tapped on his watch to signal time was about up.

She kissed her father on the cheek and stood. Her disappointment felt like a brick in her chest. "I love you, Daddy. Always have. Always will." She didn't expect him to say it back to her. No, her father's way of saying he loved someone was through things. That's what her little car had been about.

Sheridan walked around his chair to leave, but he caught her hand. She met the pleading in his eyes and waited.

"I'm proud of you, Sheri. I love you."

The tears she'd held back burned again. She bent down and hugged him. Maybe her father was on a journey to discovering the more important things in life now like she had.

His lawyer opened the door to a throng of reporters gathered in the hallway.

"I better go. Have to get to work." Sheridan shielded her face and kept her head down as she pushed her way through the clamor. Once outside she let out a heavy breath.

If her father could face what lay ahead, surely she could face Noah and his father and tell them the truth.

Maybe he'd forgive her like she had her father, or maybe he'd ask her to leave. Either way, she knew one thing. She couldn't continue lying.

---

She invaded his dreams through the night just as she'd invaded his heart. The way she felt in his arms and returned his kiss. He wanted a future with her.

But something in his gut told him he may have to fight for Sheridan. Though he didn't have a clue why, he could tell she kept something deep and hidden from him. That realization had made the night fitful as well. Brought out that need to rescue her, which also triggered his cautious, burned-by-experience side.

A puddle could be deeper than it looked.

He rose in the morning feeling like he did back in college after an all-nighter studying or the morning after the party to celebrate the end of exam week. Maybe he should just ask her what was going on, but that felt more like a violation of her privacy. He should let her know if she ever needed help to not hesitate to ask. Maybe then she'd be more open about the shadow he glimpsed lurking in her eyes sometimes.

Noah tossed his toothbrush into the cup by the sink. Or he could keep his mouth shut and let her be. Probably the wiser decision. Why did relationships have to be so complicated? If he really cared for her, he should just be honest with her and express his concern.

He clicked on his shaver. Cared for her? That felt like the understatement of the year. He'd never felt drawn to any woman like he was to Sheridan. But he also didn't want his desire to help her—rescue her—to muddle his feelings.

*Call it what it is, Noah. You want to rescue the girl.*

As he approached the kitchen, he heard dishes clanking. His heart sped in anticipation of seeing Sheridan. But only his father stood at the sink, loading the dishwasher. He swung his gaze to the dinette but found it empty of her presence as well. No coffee started yet either.

He grabbed the glass carafe and shoved it under the running water. "Where's Sheridan?"

His father didn't look at him, just kept his head hanging down. "She left early."

"That's right. She said she had a coffee date with her father."

"I don't think it was a coffee date." His father picked up his iPad and handed it to him. His father liked to read the news online and catch breaking news as well. This one read *Local Business Tycoon Pleads Guilty*.

He scrolled up to see the rest of the page. A large picture of Randall Scott sitting with a young woman attributed to be Sheridan Lane Scott filled the screen.

No mistaking the name *or* the resemblance. He handed the iPad back to his father and shoved the pot into the machine. His mother was right—his Messiah complex had blinded him once again.

His father put a hand on his arm. "I'm sure she has a good explanation."

He unclenched his jaw and swallowed down the lump of anger sitting in his throat. "What explanation could she have for not telling us who she really is? She knew what happened to you—what her father did to you. And she worked for him! She knew all this time what he did to you, even lived in my house, and lied the entire time."

"The article doesn't say anything about her involvement. I don't think she knew about it."

"Doesn't matter. She still lied."

His father gestured at the iPad. "Don't forget that she lost her home in all this too. You need to hear her side of the story, Son."

How could his father so easily let this go? "You sound like you've forgiven her already?"

"Nothing to forgive until I know the full story and all I know right now is she wound up with nothing, just like I did. You sure she wasn't just as much a victim of her father's actions as I was?"

Noah let the possibility sink in that Sheridan had suffered too. But that didn't change one thing. "She didn't say anything when I offered her the room to rent. Not even when she found out you lost your savings thanks to that sc—. How could I ever trust her?"

His father rested a hand on his shoulder. "That's something only you can decide."

# Chapter Thirteen

Sheridan sat in Noah's office, waiting to go over her latest ideas with him. But first, she had to tell Noah who she really was. News had already leaked about her father's plea change and she'd hid from the truth long enough.

Her heart hurt at the thought. Once he found out who she was, would he believe that she never meant to mislead him or his father? That she'd not only grown to love both of them, but had fallen in love with Noah…like she'd never fallen before.

Ever…

Everything about him inspired her to do better. To be a better person. He'd captured her heart that first day when he cleaned the wine off of her feet, and every interaction since had pulled her deeper into a hope that she could have a real life again. A better, more meaningful one…maybe even with him.

"Sheridan." Noah strode into the office but he didn't sit down.

She shot up from her seat. His expression matched his

tone—somber. Something was definitely wrong. And why wouldn't he look at her? Did he know already?

"Noah, I need to tell you—"

He held his hand out. "I already know."

Mouth dry and heart pounding, she forced the words out in a rough whisper. "I'm so sorry. I never meant—"

"Why didn't you tell just tell me?"

"I wanted to, but when I found out about your father, I didn't know how."

The silence in the room screamed at her as she waited for him to sit down or speak. Or do something. She felt like a child at the principal's office, waiting to be scolded.

He finally sat behind his desk. "I'm going to be honest and say I'm at a loss here."

Was he just saying that to be real or was he highlighting her dishonesty? Either way, didn't matter. She had a feeling she was going to need Emma's couch. "I didn't know what else to do."

"So you lied?" His gaze drilled into her.

"Would you have still hired me if I told you the truth right away?"

He dropped his gaze. "That's not the point."

"Isn't it? I needed a job, Noah. Sarasota is a big, small town. I didn't have a choice."

He faced her again, his expression pained. "You always have a choice, Sheridan. I just wish you'd chosen to tell the truth, especially when I rented you my guest room."

Tears sprung into her eyes. "You're right. I should have told you then." She pushed her hands under her thighs. "But I chickened out. After meeting your dad and hearing his story, I couldn't stand the idea of you two hating me."

He dragged a hand down his face. "Dad doesn't hate you. He actually defended you."

"He did?" A teeny bud of hope formed in her heart.

Noah fiddled with a pen on his desk. "And he said I should hear your side of the story."

She fought against bursting into tears. "I had no idea what my father was doing."

"Dad said the article said as much."

Was that a flash of compassion in his eyes? Would he forgive her? Could he—?

"But that doesn't change the fact that you lied to me." Anger crept into his tone.

The bud of hope wilted. Even if he forgave her, he wouldn't want to get involved with her. She could read between the lines—he didn't trust her anymore. "I'll make other living arrangements."

His jaw muscles pulsed. "I think that's a good idea."

Might as well get the whole ugly mess out there. "Would you like me to write a letter of resignation as well? That way you're covered legally?" Her voice sounded dead even to herself.

A battle seemed to wage across his face before he sighed. "No. I'm willing to keep this situation professional if you are."

Her jaw had to be sitting in her lap. "Really?"

"Yes. You're good at what you do, and I'd be a fool to let you go. But this is strictly business. Is that clear?"

"Yes." She jumped to the edge of her seat. More time would allow her to prove herself, and regain his trust too. "Thank you. I promise I'll do a good job. I love working here."

With a nod, he glanced away. No more lingering looks. He didn't seem to want to look at her at all.

She stood and headed toward the door.

"Sheridan."

The sound of her name on his lips was like a splash of water to her wilted hope. "Yeah?"

"Close the door behind you." He still didn't look at her, just kept his eyes on the computer screen.

She hated that he wouldn't look at her. Made her heart ache even more than finding out her father really had embezzled all those people out of their retirement funds. Noah had been the first person to really see her for who she was—not some spoiled rich girl whose Daddy turned out to be a thief.

Now she was nothing to him too. "Sure, no problem."

The click of his door matched the sound of her hope falling to the ground. No care and feeding would bring that bud back to life.

---

Once he knew Sheridan was no longer outside the door, he smacked his hand on the desk. The blotter helped muffle the sound but not enough to keep Manny from poking his head in the door. "Everything okay in here?"

"Just fine and dandy, Manny." Elbows on the desk, he held his head in his hands and closed his eyes.

"You sure about that, Noah?" Manny thought it was funny to call him 'Boss' even though they'd been friends long before Manny came to work for him, but he would always use Noah's name when speaking as his friend.

"Yeah, I'll be fine. Just a complication."

Manny glanced in the direction Sheridan disappeared. "She's a pretty amazing complication."

"You don't know the half of it."

Stepping into the office, Manny shut the door. "I saw

the news. All of us did. Sheridan looked pretty messed up when she came in this morning."

"Did she say anything to you?"

"No, just came straight to your office. Did you let her go?"

"No, but maybe I should have."

"Nah, that's not your style."

"Yeah, tell me about it. Just hope I don't live to regret it."

Hands in his pants pockets, Manny looked at a loss for words.

"I'm fine, Man. Don't worry."

"Okay." He paused at the door. "You know where to find me if you want to talk."

"Thanks." Once the door closed, he pushed back the hair on his forehead and leaned back in his chair.

Fool. He must have that tattooed on his forehead. Anyone else would have accepted her resignation out of relief to get rid of the tangled mess. Stickier than day-old pasta noodles. Why hadn't he accepted her offer to resign?

The resignation settled in that he couldn't save everyone. And he accepted it this time. Sheridan had been his last attempt, but that recipe had failed miserably—again. No permanent place on the menu for that one. And he was better off knowing now before he'd invested his heart fully.

His father would be pleased to hear he hadn't fired her. Seeing her every day would be difficult though. At least she wouldn't be in his home anymore. He didn't think his resolve could withstand that. His attraction and draw to her still waged a war with his common sense.

A knock came from the door. He steeled himself in case Sheridan had returned. "Come in."

Sara walked in, dressed in gray, pinstripe slacks and a

fitted jacket to match. Very professional and crisp. She'd stepped into her assistant manager role more diligently than he'd expected. "Can I talk to you for a minute?"

He waved to the chair Sheridan just vacated. "Sure."

She sat, careful to arrange herself in the seat before looking at him. "I'm sure you saw the news by now."

Closed his eyes. Deep breath. Exhale. How much fallout would this situation generate? He leaned forward, crossing his hands on this desk. "Yep, perfectly aware, and it's been dealt with."

Sara lifted a manicured hand and swept it toward the door like one of those models at a weekend car show. And with all the attitude to match. "And yet she's still here." She dropped her hand to her knee. "Do you think that's wise?"

"Like I said, I dealt with it. Sheridan is good at what she does. She didn't have anything to do with her father's actions, so I see no need to penalize her for them."

She tilted her head at him. "They say 'acorns don't fall far from the tree' for a reason."

A laugh bigger than Mount Vesuvius threatened to explode out of him. "Yes, Sara, and in your case, that is clearly true."

She jerked her head back in confusion and her eyes glazed as she tried to figure out if he'd complimented or insulted her.

Best not to poke the bear…

"Don't worry about it, okay? I will keep an eye on things. But if you hear anything I should be concerned about, don't hesitate to let me know."

She smiled as she stood. "Not a problem."

After she left, he tried to work on the order for the following week, but his mind kept drifting to Sheridan, still trying to make sense of her actions. He wanted nothing more than to brush off the entire situation and go back to how things were before his heart had engaged.

He dragged his mind back to the spreadsheet just in time to see that he'd almost ordered ten cases of grapefruit from one of the local farmers. Chef Margot would annihilate him for that one. He closed the screen. Right now he needed to clear his head.

Noah went out the back door of the restaurant, strode down Pineapple Avenue, and then headed to Five Points. Walking the circle cleared his head and connected him back to the hum of downtown Sarasota. He loved the tall buildings, especially the Plaza. He stopped in front of the fountain and fished a quarter from his pocket. His wish needed more than a penny, for sure.

As he was about to toss it in, his cell buzzed in his pocket. He pulled it out and hesitated to answer when he saw Lancaster's name at the top. Sara must have called her father and tattled on him.

He accepted the call. "What can I do for you, Jordan?"

"I hear you're letting criminals work at the restaurant."

"If you're referring to Sheridan, she isn't a criminal, nor has she done anything wrong."

"Don't forget guilt by association, Noah."

He resisted the urge to toss his phone into the fountain instead of the quarter. "What do you want, Jordan?"

"Fire Sheridan. It's bad for business. You know that."

"I know nothing of the sort. Sheridan is great at what she does. Madilyn's needs her."

"Madilyn's needs her or you need her?"

"What are you implying?"

The sound of Jordan's exhale bled over the line. "Sara seems to think Sheridan has…deeper interests."

The light bulb went on. "Jordan, is this about the restaurant or your daughter?"

"Why can't it be both?"

If the world could hear Noah's inward groan, they'd think they just heard the alarm signaling the end of the world. "Madilyn's is my restaurant, Jordan. I made that clear when I accepted your investment. I can't run the place just to make your daughter happy. That's not good for business either."

"True, but if you and Sara were back together, then it would be a joint venture."

Every muscle in his body stiffened. "As I recall, Sara was the one who ended the relationship. I don't think she'd appreciate you meddling with her love life."

"My daughter has never been very good at knowing what's best for her, Noah. But I do, and you are good for her. If you two were back together, say even engaged...then my investment would turn into a gift."

Classic. Jordan's manipulating MO had now turned into bribery. The man had to be nuts. "Sara would be livid if she knew what you were trying to do."

"Oh, I'm aware of that, but I'm confident you'd never do anything to activate that little addendum I asked you to add to our agreement. In case you forgot, let me remind you that if at any time I feel the need to pull out or feel things are not being managed well, my investment would be considered a loan payable *in full*, immediately."

Noah remembered *full* well. He'd accepted the terms based upon his assumption that since he was dating his daughter, Jordan had pure motivations, for the most part. But his desperation had made him reckless. If he hadn't jumped on the deal, he would have lost the restaurant. That had probably blinded him to many things at the time.

"So, are we clear?"

Threat received loud and clear.

He could take the easy way out and tell Sheridan he had to accept her resignation after all. If he told her about the pressure Lancaster had put upon him, she'd probably tell him she'd leave right away. He didn't miss the lingering guilt in her eyes.

But despite his anger—and disappointment if he was going to be totally honest with himself—he couldn't do that to her.

"Crystal. But let me be clear as well. I have no legal grounds to fire Sheridan Lane. And you probably know better than most what legal entanglements could arise, especially in light of the circumstances surrounding her father's case."

Though not entirely certain about the accuracy of his counter-argument, Noah refused to back down. He believed Sheridan had no part in what her father did. Didn't fit her character, although winding up nearly homeless could turn someone around to make better choices.

Or…make them desperate…

No, his main issue was that Sheridan had lived in his house under a lie. She'd shown herself exemplary in the workplace. And, if he were to continue to be brutally honest with his inner self, he still cared about her.

"Fine." Jordan's expelled breath filtered through. "You're a good man, Noah. I know you'll do the right thing when it's necessary."

The connection ended. Was that a compliment or another one of Jordan's carefully couched manipulations?

Noah dropped the phone into his pocket. He flipped the quarter in his hand and changed his wish before tossing it into the fountain.

## Chapter Fourteen

Sheridan leaned against her car as she waited for Kaleena to come out the back door. She'd wanted to run over and talk to her all day, but the plans for their new lunch seating had to be finalized, and then the restaurant had been busier than usual in the evening, which meant no dinner break for her.

Had Kaleena seen the story? How could she not have? The woman seemed to have her finger on the pulse of everyone on Pineapple Avenue. Not in a bad or gossipy way. She just seemed to know what all the hum was about.

The door swung open, but Evelyn walked out to dump a bag into the dumpster. Sheridan crossed the parking lot and met her there. "Hey, Evelyn. Is Kaleena still inside?"

After tossing the bag over the side, Evelyn turned to face her. "Yeah, she's still there."

Sheridan pointed toward the door. "Okay if I go in and say hello?"

Evelyn shrugged. "I suppose."

She didn't know if Evelyn still didn't like her because of

that first encounter in the shop or if the woman had seen the news and now had even more reason to dislike Miss Snooty Pants. Didn't matter. Right now she was more concerned about where she stood with Kaleena. Her BFF Emma already knew all her business and still loved her despite it all. That's what they did for each other, and though her friendship with Kaleena seemed to be heading in the closer-than-most direction, she hadn't known her long enough to know how she'd react.

Sheridan followed Evelyn through the dressing room area into the shop. Kaleena stood behind the counter, staring at the computer screen.

"Miss Snooty Pants is here to see you, Kay."

Well, one question answered…

Kaleena turned her head as she put one hand on her hip. "Is she now?"

Evelyn raised her eyebrows at Kaleena who responded likewise.

Sheridan waited for Evelyn to go back the way they came before moving to lean on the counter. "Is Kay your nickname?"

Kaleena stared at her long enough to make the room feel suffocating. "Is that how you want to start this conversation because I think there's a bigger secret in the room." She grabbed some papers from the other side of the register and smacked them down on the counter in front of Sheridan. A printout of a news article breaking the news about her father.

An image of her sitting with her father that morning stared back at her. She sighed. "That's why I'm here. I wanted to tell you before, but—"

"You didn't. Why?" Kaleena frowned at her but appeared concerned too.

Mustering her courage, she pulled her shoulders up and held her hands out. "I was afraid you'd think I was somehow involved and dump me like most of my other friends had."

"Now why would you think I'd do that?"

She lifted one brow. "Miss Snooty Pants?"

Kaleena dropped her chin before tilting her head. "Okay, you got me there, but let me explain to you something about Kaleena Brooks. Once a friend, always a friend." She wagged her hand between them. "And we're friends. Or so I thought."

Sheridan didn't bother to stop the tears from streaming down her cheeks. "We are most definitely friends."

Kaleena hustled around the counter and wrapped her arms around Sheridan in a big bear hug. "I've been waiting all day to do that. I can't even imagine what you must be feeling right now."

Once Kaleena let go, she wiped her cheeks. "Oh, it's worse actually."

Kaleena tapped the newspaper. "Seriously? Worse than that?"

She nodded. "Noah's dad is one of the people my father embezzled from." There, she said it…admitted it. Her father was a criminal. The waterworks turned on again.

"Oh, sweet Lord." Kaleena didn't say another word. Just hugged her tight again and didn't let go while she bawled on her shoulder.

"Good night, Kay…what the…?"

Sheridan pulled back. "Sorry."

"It's all good, Evelyn. Sheri here just needs some TLC. I'll close the rest up."

Evelyn shifted her gaze from Kaleena to Sheridan, hesitated to say something, then strode over and gave Sheridan a hug. "I always say the morning will have the answers I need. And it will all work out better than I expect."

Kaleena held her hand out. "See? There you go."

A soft giggle burst out of Sheridan. She sniffled and accepted the tissues Kaleena handed her. "Thank you, ladies. I'm so grateful for your encouragement." She started crying again.

"You got this, Kay? Beni's waiting for me."

"You go on." She waved Evelyn on.

Sheridan blew her nose. "Who's Beni?"

"Benjamin. That's Evelyn's little boy. Her mother watches him in the evenings so she can work."

"She's a single mom?"

"Yes, ma'am. And a great one too."

She nodded as a new appreciation for Evelyn bloomed in her heart. A series of hiccups accompanied her exhale. "Life is hard."

"Ain't that the truth, but that's why we do it together." Kaleena gave her a pointed stare to bring home her point.

Sheridan felt like she was going to start bawling again. "I'm sorry I wasn't honest with you. I really don't deserve your friendship."

"Sweetie, you don't have to earn my friendship. I freely give it. And I completely understand, especially in light of all the rejection you've gone through because of your father. But if you don't mind me saying this, a friend who dumps you in your time of need is no friend of yours indeed."

Sheridan laughed at the twist of an old saying. "That's really good. And true."

Kaleena broke into a big smile. "Evelyn's right. Things will look better in the morning. I'm sure of it."

She wanted to believe that more than anything at the

moment. How much more heartache could she take and not crumble? "Thank you, Kaleena."

"For what?"

"For still being my friend."

"Of course. Whatever you need."

"Can I ask a favor then?"

"Anything."

Sheridan glanced down, then back to meet her friend's dark brown eyes and the compassion that filled them. "Can I call you Kay?"

Kaleena's eyes grew moist this time. "Of course, Sheri. I'd be glad if you did."

She hugged Kay again, blew her nose, and then fished in her purse for her phone. "Now to call another friend and see if I can use her couch. I told Noah I'd find someplace else to stay."

"Seriously? He's making you leave?"

"No, I offered."

"And he agreed?"

"He said it was probably for the best." She lifted one shoulder and swiped away a rogue tear. If only life had an undo button like computers. Working near Noah would be brutal but the thought of never seeing him again seemed worse. "He was pretty upset that I didn't tell him the truth."

Kay shook her head. "That man doesn't know a good thing when he sees it."

Though it sounded like Kay was talking to herself, Sheridan couldn't help but be curious. "What do you mean?"

Kay snapped her smile back in place. "Nothing you need to worry about. Why don't you stay with me for a while? I have an extra bedroom."

As much as the idea appealed to her—and seemed

almost providential—Sheridan didn't want to bring her trail of woes and complications into her new friend's life. "No, I couldn't do that to you, Kay."

"What are you talking about? It'll be fun. You'll see. It's not like you'll be the first friend who's ever stayed with me. Oh, the stories my spare room could tell you. Even Evelyn and Beni stayed with me for a time."

"Really? Are you sure?"

"Of course I am. I wouldn't offer it if I didn't mean it."

As much as she loved hanging out at Emma's place, a room beat a couch any day. "Okay then. And I'm happy to pay you rent."

Kay laughed and waved her off. "Let's see if you like living with me first. Then we can discuss terms."

Sheridan held her hand out. "Deal."

---

Noah lingered in the kitchen, going over the plans for the lunch seating and promotions that would release throughout the week. At least, that was his excuse for still being up. He didn't like the way he left things with Sheridan earlier today, and she'd ducked out as soon as her shift was over.

He checked his watch again. Had she decided to stay somewhere else tonight? As much as he wanted to make friends with his bed at the moment, he needed to know she was safe first.

His phone sat nearby...he could text her and just ask. But he couldn't bring himself to do it. Just felt too personal and that was exactly what he needed to avoid.

The sound of the key in the front door alerted him to her arrival first. He stayed in the kitchen and continued his guise of busyness. Once she went into her room, he'd turn in as well.

The click of her heels preceded her arrival into the kitchen. She appeared as uneasy as he felt, the way she kept glancing down at the car keys in her hands. "You're still up."

Her statement brought a flash of déjà vu. The last time she'd said that the evening ended with a passionate kiss at her bedroom door. "Just wrapping my head around what the week ahead will entail."

"Anything I can do to help?"

When he met her gaze to answer her, he lost his ability to speak. The plea in her eyes made him want to dump everything he'd decided about her and pull her into his arms. His lips even tingled at the thought. And the memory of their last kiss did nothing to help his resistance.

He cleared his throat and refocused on the papers in front of him. "No, I'm just about done." He kept his head down, waiting for her to leave, but she didn't. And he didn't raise his head. He'd get caught in those dark eyes and forget everything and anything sensible in this situation.

Her keys jingled. "Well, goodnight then. I'll have my things out in the morning."

As she turned to leave, he finally let himself catch a glimpse of her but couldn't seem to let go. Not yet. "Did you find a place to stay?"

She stepped back into the kitchen. "I'm going to stay with Kaleena. Turns out she has a spare bedroom and no roommate at the moment. So we're going to give it a try."

He should be relieved but he wasn't. More like disappointed, but what else could he do in this no-win situation? "Good. I'm glad. Kaleena is great."

"Yeah, she's become a really good friend." Tears pooled

in her eyes. "I'm really sorry, Noah. I hope at some point you'll be able to forgive me."

He wanted to more than anything, wanted to be that kind of person. And he hated that he wasn't. What could he say to her? "I want to, Sheridan, I really do. Maybe over time."

She nodded and then disappeared out the doorway again. Only the fading tap of her heels and the click of her door told him she'd retired for the night.

Fatigue washed over him. He dropped his head into his hands to ride the wave of emotions tearing at him from the inside out, like a kettle of water about to whistle on the burner. But he reined it in. Had too. And hatched a plan.

With Sara in charge of the lunch seating, he could create more distance between him and Sheridan. He made a note on his to-do list to shift her hours to the daytime seating so she and Sheridan would work together for the lunch seating. He'd take care of the dinner crowd until they found a greeter for that shift. That would allow only a small overlap of time where they'd both be at the restaurant. During the day he worked in the office most of the time anyway.

Satisfied with his solution, he gathered his paperwork and headed to his room. The sooner he got over Sheridan Lane Scott the better.

# Chapter Fifteen

Unable to face Noah and his father, Sheridan stayed in her room until she heard Noah leave and knew Norman would be gone playing pickleball with his friends. But packing her things brought an unexpected surge of emotions that landed in her chest and stayed there. She'd grown to not only love Noah, but his quirky father too. Though he couldn't cook anything edible, the man certainly knew how the wield a paintbrush.

She opened her bedroom door and listened, but the house remained silent. Once she had her things packed, she'd head to Kaleena's and drop them off before going to work. Kaleena gave her a quick tour last night. Her place was warm and cozy. She'd even have her own bathroom.

Sheridan returned to the foot of the bed and stared at the painting that had captured her heart her first night here. She felt like that girl again, facing a forest of the unknown and preparing to venture in. How she wished she could have stayed here, in Noah Kent's forest.

She shoved a stack of her belongings into the suitcase. "Oh, well."

"Oh, well what?" Norman's voice came from behind her.

She spun around. "Norman...I thought you were playing pickleball."

He tucked his hands into the pockets of his painting overalls. "Nah, didn't feel like running around a court. Been out back painting."

"Oh, that's nice." She sank down on the edge of the bed.

Norman gestured at her suitcase. "You're really leaving?"

She nodded and braved a smile she didn't feel. "It's for the best."

Dropping his hands to his sides, he stepped into the doorway. "Do you have a place to stay?"

She stood and went back to loading her suitcase. Easier if he didn't see her face. "I'm going to stay with Kaleena. I think you know her."

"The one who owns the clothing shop?"

"Yeah, that's her."

A sad and distant smile slid into his expression. "I used to find gifts for my wife there."

Her eyes burned but she fought the tears forming. She'd not add to this man's misery any more than her father already had. "She was one lucky woman."

He puckered his lips, which pushed his nose up and wrinkled his forehead. "I told Noah you didn't have anything to do with what happened and that I understood why you didn't tell us who you really are."

She jumped to close the distance between them and put

her hand on his arm. "I am so sorry for what my father did to you."

"Sheridan, that's not your job."

"But I feel so bad." She swallowed down a sudden rush of tears that would have had her sobbing on the floor. Not seeing Norman anymore would be almost as hard as working with Noah and not being able to get close to him.

He took her hand. "You are not responsible for your father's actions, so it's not your job to apologize. Even when I found out who you really are, I didn't hold you accountable. You were a victim in this as much as I was."

This time she let the tears fall as she nodded. "I'm just so embarrassed."

Norman pulled her into a hug. "I know, but life has a beautiful way of going on, even in the worst of our circumstances."

"That doesn't seem fair though." She sniffled as she leaned back.

"Fair has nothing to do with it. It's about possibilities. I know things may seem bleak right now, but you are at the precipice of new possibilities."

She turned to look at his painting over the bed. "Kind of like her?"

He broke into a wide grin. "Exactly. I painted that one for Madilyn when Noah went off to college. She said she felt lost in a sea of trees. So painted what I imagined she saw, but with light behind the trees to hint at the possibilities waiting for her."

Sheridan walked over to the head of the bed to get closer to the painting. She reached out and touched the figure of the woman. "So that's Madilyn?"

"Yes, and that's you too, Sheridan. A forest of possibilities is there, waiting for you to explore."

She swallowed down another round of tears as she ran over and wrapped Norman in another hug. He felt like the father she'd always wanted. "Thank you."

"For what?"

"For being so good and kind." She let out a slobbery laugh as she stepped back. "Noah is just like you, you know. So kind and caring."

Norman studied her, then nodded. "He loves you too, you know."

His words almost took her breath away. Was she that obvious? And could what Norman said be true? Everything in her wanted to believe that, but part of her hoped it wasn't. Because that would feel like an even bigger loss.

She loaded the last pile of her belongings and closed the zipper. After lowering her suitcase to the floor, she pulled out her cell phone and took a picture of the painting. "I'm going to look at this every time I'm discouraged or sad."

He didn't say anything, just gave her a wan smile.

She grabbed her bag. "Thank you, Norman." She kissed his cheek and then walked as fast as she could out of the house to her car.

The sooner she left the better. She didn't think her heart could take any more pain.

---

In need of a double shot iced coffee from Java Jerry's, Noah left his office and headed to the front of the restaurant. The first two weeks of the new lunch seating had nearly doubled their numbers. And thanks to a big yearly arts and crafts event happening downtown, this weekend's numbers would put those to shame.

He had enough time to walk down to the coffee shop

and get some specialized fuel before the surplus food shipments he'd ordered arrived. That alone would keep him busy through the rest of the morning. Plus he had to set up the table and chairs he brought back from his house in addition to three others he'd ordered, which arrived yesterday. Business had expanded faster than he expected.

As much as he hated to admit it, his plan had worked. Sara had managed a fair bit of the daytime operations, allowing him to come in later or stay in his office to work on other things. So far, she'd proved to have gleaned some of her father's business acumen. And he'd managed to interact with Sheridan only when necessary.

As he passed through the front of the restaurant, he spotted her standing outside Kaleena's shop. As much as it pained both him and his father to not have Sheridan around the house anymore, he was glad she'd found a good and safe place to land. Part of him still cringed at his inability to move past her deception and give her another chance—but he didn't fire her and even defended her when Lancaster tried to manipulate him into letting her go. That must count for something.

Yet all his self-justification did nothing to take away the heaviness he felt whenever he saw her. He had no doubt she knew he was avoiding her. How could she not? But how else could he keep things professional between them when his heart still played traitor in his plan to get over her.

He felt Sheridan's eyes on him as he walked to the coffee shop across the street, but he'd kept his attention forward. The less he engaged with her the better. He had to give his heart time to detangle and keeping his distance was the only way he knew how to do that without asking her to leave the restaurant too.

If she had just been honest with him…

But as she pointed out, would he have hired her if she had told him? Would he have listened beyond his own anger over how her father's deceit affected his father—his life too for that matter? And if he had hired her out of the 'goodness' of his misguided heart, would he have turned a blind eye and let her sleep in her car that night?

He joined the line at the ordering counter, standing just inside the door. Several people sat with their Java Jerry cups, reading the newspaper. Sheridan and her family stared back at him from a few of the tables. He groaned. The story just wouldn't die off.

Who knew separating Sheridan from her father would prove so difficult? But he wasn't mad at her for what happened with her father. He was mad at her for lying to him about who she was and letting him fall in love with her.

Wait…what?

"You look like you just saw a ghost."

The comment pulled his attention back from the gut punch that came with realizing he loved Sheridan. When had that happened and how could he fall for someone that fast? He gave his head a quick shake and focused on the short woman nearby. "Oh, hey, Kaleena. Didn't hear you come in."

"Are you okay?" She tucked her chin and eyed him. "You look a little pale."

He paused, considered what to say since Kaleena and Sheridan were now roommates. "Did Sheridan send you to check on me?"

"No, but I'm guessing that pained look on your face is related to her." She nailed him with a telling look.

His insides started to squirm. "What makes you say that?"

"Because I saw how hard you tried not to look at her."

He closed his eyes and tilted his head back before shooting his question at her. "Was it that obvious?"

"Honey, you know Kaleena Brooks doesn't miss a thing that happens on Pineapple Avenue." She laughed at her admission.

"Then you know more than me." He regretted the words the minute they came out.

She drew her brows together in a frown. "Sometimes you have to give a person the benefit of the doubt. Can't always be cut-and-dried. You know, extenuating circumstances and all that."

Noah lifted one side of his mouth and snorted. "You sound like my father."

She swatted him on the shoulder, her grin widening. "How is that ole' sweetheart doing? I haven't seen Norman since…" Her smile fell into a concerned frown. "Well, since your mama died. He used to come in every so often to buy something special for her."

"He's still living with me. And painting again. I set up a studio for him in the old sunroom in the back of my place."

She patted his arm. "You are a good man, Noah Kent."

He muttered his reply. "So I've been told."

"That's what I love about you. You have a good heart. Always helping others when you can. Including Sheridan. Giving her a job and a place to live."

"But she lied to me." Raw emotions pushed the words out before he'd had time to consider them. Several people looked his way, making him realize he'd raised his voice. "Sorry."

This time Kaleena stared at him with concern. "I know this is a difficult situation to navigate. Sheridan told me about how your dad was affected too."

"She told you?" He felt the jab that Sheridan would confide in Kaleena but not him.

"Yeah. She was afraid I was going to reject her like all her other friends did when all this hullabaloo started." She waved her hand toward the sea of newspaper readers. "Yeah, that girl's life has been a sea of hurt. First, her dad is arrested and charged with embezzlement. Then she loses her job and her condo, which she was paying for herself, I might add. *And then* her friends reject her and her mother runs away. The only thing she had left was her little car, which she loves because it was a gift from her father. Although who knows how she feels about it now in light of her father's confession."

"Wow, that's a lot." *Aaaaand* now he felt like a jerk. He'd made Sheridan's lie about him. He never stopped to think about what would push her to that point.

"That's what I was saying." Eyes wide, she bobbed her head.

He knew Sheridan had lost her condo, but he didn't know about the rest of what she'd endured. Through the loss of his mother and then his father having to move in with him, he'd only considered his own pain and suffering.

He needed to talk to Sheridan. "I need to go."

"What about your coffee? I can bring it by if you'd like. Just tell me what you want."

"No, that's okay. What I really want isn't on the menu here."

Kaleena gave him a knowing smile. "I thought that might be the case."

Noah strode back to the restaurant, rehearsing in his mind what he would say to Sheridan. That he forgave her? Did he? He realized now that he loved her. But was that enough?

The beeping sound of the first delivery truck backing in met him as he strode into the front door of the restaurant. Several servers and staff had come in early to help get the additional tables set up and help Chef stock the kitchen. But no sign of Sheridan and she was usually in the thick of things, especially regarding the lunch seating.

He didn't find her in the kitchen either so he went straight to his office.

Sara sat at the desk he'd set up for her on the other side of the small office—her cubby, as she called it.

"Where's Sheridan?" He glanced toward the back door where Margot and Manny were overseeing the delivery but didn't see her there either.

Sara clasped her hands in front of her. "I had to let her go."

He shot his gaze to her. "What do you mean?"

She plucked a stack of papers from her desk and held them out to him. "I went over the invoices for the last two weeks and found a five thousand dollar discrepancy."

Every muscle in his body went on high alert as his pulse sped. "So you assumed it was Sheridan."

"She certainly had good reason. The poor girl is penniless, thanks to her father. And desperate. People can surprise you in that kind of situation."

He took the papers and scanned the first and second pages. Red ink highlighted various numbers.

"The invoices don't match the payments. You know the saying about apples. Or was it acorns?" She held a finely manicured nail to her mouth as she looked upward to some imaginary source.

"You should have consulted with me first, Sara. We need to look into this first before making any accusations."

She sauntered over to him and tapped the top button of

his shirt with the same finger. "I knew your feelings for her would cloud your judgment, so I took care of it for you."

Manny shouted from the back, asking for a sign-off for the delivery.

"Can you take care of that, please?"

"Of course. That's what I'm here for." She swaggered by him, leaving a trail of her overwhelming perfume. Or was that smug satisfaction he smelled?

He resisted the urge the slam his office door after she left, and the click of the lock did nothing to assuage his anger. Hands fisted at his sides, he spun around, looking for something to punch or kick. Though Sheridan's charts still covered the top of the whiteboard, her implementation bullet points had all been erased. Most likely Sara's work as well. She wanted to erase Sheridan's presence completely.

Noah dropped into his chair and ran his hands into his hair, then leaned his elbows on the desk. A corner of a piece of paper poked out from under his desk calendar. He tugged it out and unfolded it.

*Noah, I am not like my father.*

She signed her note with just an 'S.'

Had he dodged a bullet or had he lost the best thing that had come into his life in a long time? Even desperate, he couldn't imagine Sheridan doing something like stealing from the restaurant. There had to be another explanation.

Noah grabbed the stack of invoices and flipped through them again, following her trail of red circles and lines to show the discrepancy. The delivery receipts had Sheridan's signature. And Sara was right, the numbers didn't add up.

But he struggled to believe she could do something like this. Sheridan said she loved working at Madilyn's, loved her job.

He glanced at her note again, then crumpled and tossed

it onto his desk. Whether he could forgive Sheridan or not had nothing to do with finding out the truth. No way would she steal from the restaurant.

But he had a suspicion about who might have. Now if he could prove it.

## Chapter Sixteen

Sheridan wiggled her toes into the cool sand—one of the things she loved most about Siesta Key Beach. Made of quartz, the sand stayed cool even on the hottest days. And today was one of them. With a sigh, she sat back in her beach chair. The shade of the umbrella cooled her hot skin.

"Happy birthday, Sheri." Emma handed her a diet soda and a package of chocolate cupcakes. The cheap kind with the white braid on top.

Her secret indulgence as a teenager had become all she could afford these days. She snatched the package from her best friend. "You remembered!"

Emma laughed. "Are you kidding? How could I forget? Our dorm room garbage can was always filled with wrappers from those things."

Sheridan swiped a finger into the cream filling and popped it into her mouth. "These things got me through exams."

"I know." Emma rubbed more suntan lotion on her legs. "How's the job searching going, by the way?"

She finished the last bit of her first cupcake. "Nothing yet. I'm hoping all the press will die down soon and people will start forgetting who I am."

"Except for one hunky restaurant owner, I'm guessing."

She folded over the package to save the other one for later. "Not likely."

"Why not? You're quite unforgettable, Sheridan Lane Scott."

She rolled her eyes. "That's not a compliment."

Pulling her sunglasses down, Emma leaned over the side of her chair to get her attention. "Yes, it is. You're amazing. Why can't you see that?"

"Uh, hello? Jobless, homeless, and no prospects."

"That's just your circumstances, not who you are." Emma always did have a way of reminding her of the truth.

"Thank you. But I haven't a clue of what to do next. I love marketing, but who wants to hire the daughter of an embezzler?"

"Their loss."

She smiled her appreciation for her friend's support. "Love the sentiment, dear heart, but that does not pay the bills." She sighed. "Kaleena told me not to worry about paying any rent until I get a job, but I think I'm going to have to sell my car."

Emma looked at her as if she'd sprouted a second head. "What?! No way. You love that car."

"I know, I do…did. But I need the money more so I can get back on my feet. I can always walk or take the bus."

Emma leaned back and pushed her sunglasses back in place. "Something will come along. I'm sure of it."

Sheridan tugged her cell phone from her bag to check her email for any interview requests that may have come in since she checked an hour ago. She scrolled through several spammy ones and stopped at one that rang alarm bells.

From her attorney. What new repercussions would she have to face now, thanks to her father? She opened the email and read the first two lines, then squealed.

Emma jerked so hard her sunglasses went flying into the sand. "What on earth?"

Sheridan wagged her hand at her. "My attorney said part of my trust fund was released! Turns out it was funded from an inheritance that was my grandmother's. The Feds couldn't touch it."

"See? I told you something would come along."

She scanned the rest of the email. "It's not a lot but enough to get me back on my feet." An unexpected thought bumped its way into the plans already flying through her head. She looked up at Emma. "And maybe enough to make amends."

---

Now he had his proof. His father said he should call the police, but Noah didn't see the point since it wasn't a huge amount of money. Besides, he had a better idea. He sat at one of the outdoor tables, waiting for Jordan and Sara to arrive. If this didn't get the Lancasters out of his hair—and his restaurant—he'd play the police card.

The heavy scent of Sara's perfume reached him before she did. He pushed a smile in place as he rose from his chair. Jordan swaggered up next to her, like the proud father he must picture himself to be. Sara walked next to him, like an identical, female younger twin.

He nodded at Sara and shook Jordan's hand. "Thank you for coming." He gestured to the table. "Please sit."

Sara scooted her chair to the table. "I hope this is worth calling me in on my day off."

"It's important. Trust me."

Jordan raised a brow at his tone.

Before the man could say anything, Noah laid out his spreadsheets on the table to give them a clearer picture of the importance of his called meeting. By the time he finished, Sara squirmed more than the toddler in a high-chair ready to get down. And her face had turned as red as the sunburned woman who just walked by.

Jordan held his hand out. "What's all this?"

"My proof." Noah waited for Jordan to catch on.

He sneered and shrugged all at once. "Of what? That you keep spreadsheets of all your orders and output?"

"Follow the trail, Jordan." Noah pointed at the bottom line.

"You have a discrepancy."

"Yep, about five grand's worth."

"Then you better get with your assistant manager on that." He darted proud papa eyes to his daughter.

Noah almost felt bad about shattering the man's perceptions of his daughter—almost. "Exactly my thought. Especially since Sara was the one who oversaw these deliveries for the lunch seating."

"Sara, do you know anything about this?"

She leaned forward, pulling one of the pages to look more closely. "Yes, I brought this to Noah's attention when I fired Sheridan Lane for stealing money from the restaurant. I thought we dealt with this already."

Noah pulled the first set of invoices. "These are the invoices we have on file from our vendors."

Jordan tapped one of the pages. "Noah, what's your point?"

Noah laid out the invoices from the actual deliveries—copies he was able to get from his vendors. "Those are your signatures, Sara, correct?"

Sara appeared as irritated as her father. "I don't like what you're implying, Noah. In case you've forgotten, Sheridan and I worked closely on the planning and orders for the lunch seating."

He pushed the pages closer to her. "*Are* those your signatures?"

She barely glanced at the documents before giving him a scathing look. "They look like my signature, but she could have forged my name. She is the daughter of an embezzler. I'm sure she *learned* quite a few things under her father's teaching."

"I talked to the delivery guys, who by the way, also happen to be friends of mine, and you were the one who signed for the deliveries—every time. Not Sheridan. Both confirmed that the amount they received is the amount on the original invoice. Not these forgeries." Noah leaned forward. "You set Sheridan up, Sara."

Jordan put his hand in front of Sara. "How dare you accuse my daughter—"

"I was just trying to prove to you that you couldn't trust that woman." Anger puckered her lips and drew her brows down, making her look even more like her father.

Sara's confession seemed to fluster Jordan for a moment. He sat back in his chair and exhaled. "Whatever's missing, I'll replace. We don't need to make a big deal out of this, do we?"

Noah unclenched his jaw. "I can agree not to go to the authorities on two conditions."

Sara jerked in her seat at his statement and her eyes turned into wide orbs of fear.

Jordan gave him a knowing look.

Noah continued, "One, Sara resigns from her position immediately. And two, you agree to convert the investment you made—minus five grand—into a loan, which I agree to pay off by the end of this calendar year."

"You sure about that, Noah? That's a chunk of change." He tilted his head and quirked his mouth, as if he thought he had the upper hand.

But Noah wouldn't tell Jordan that he'd mortgage his house if he had to. And at the rate the lunch seating was growing, he might get away with just a small second mortgage at that. "That's why you're not going to charge me interest, Jordan." Noah stacked the papers into a neat pile. "Those are my terms to keep this out of the hands of the police. I'm sure you can arrange a plan for Sara to pay you back as well."

Sara jumped up from her chair and stomped off in the direction she came.

Jordan rose to his full height, staring down at Noah.

He stood as well, waiting for Jordan to say something. Either the man would agree or make more threats. Noah hoped for the former, more for the sake of peace than anything else. He had no desire to pursue legal action.

Jordan appraised him and then relaxed his stance as he held his hand out. "Deal. As of this moment, I'm no longer an investor in Madilyn's. I'll have my attorney draw up the documents and send them over."

Noah accepted the shake and hoped it was the last one. "I'll be waiting for them."

Jordan turned to leave but paused. "I'm impressed, Noah."

He shrugged. "Why?"

"Took some guts to stand up to me like that."

"Just doing what's best for both of us, Jordan. Sara isn't a bad person."

"No, she's just spoiled. But that's on me. Not you." He gave a curt nod before walking away.

Noah inhaled and released a long breath once Jordan turned the corner. He didn't envy Sara's forthcoming conversations with her father. Maybe one day she'd figure out who she wanted to be and break away from her father's manipulations—and money.

A wave of relief washed over him and dropped him back into his chair. Dressed in her chef's jacket, Margot approached him, carrying a glass of water on a tray. She set it down in front of him. "I can bring you something stronger if you'd like."

He chuckled and gulped down half the glass. "Nope, water is perfect."

"Then I take it things went well?"

"Yes, very well. The restaurant is all mine again." He finished off his water.

Margot picked up the empty glass and put it back on her tray. "We still need an afternoon manager."

"Yeah, I know."

She arched one brow. "Got anyone in mind?"

He got her message and he agreed. Completely. "Yeah, I do actually. Let's just hope she's still available."

# Chapter Seventeen

"Any chance you can hang around? I won't be long."
Sheridan paid the Lift driver.

Dressed in board shorts and sporting a dark tan, the guy
must have the beach targeted as his ultimate destination.
"No, sorry. Already accepted another pick-up request."

The inflatable paddleboard in the back of his old SUV
confirmed her suspicions. She couldn't resist referencing
one of her favorite episodes of *Frasier*. "Mele Kalikimaka,
Bob."

"Huh? My name is Steve."

"Sorry, inside joke. Thanks anyway."

As he drove away, she clutched her purse and headed up
the walk to Noah's house. By now Norman should be back
from lunch with his buddies. And Noah would be at the
restaurant, overseeing the lunch crowd.

With Sara.

As much as she hated to think of the woman in close
proximity to Noah, she hoped the lunch seating continued
to be a huge success. She'd considered going by to see for

herself, but the thought brought out her klutzy side before she even made a decision to go. Noah had seen enough of that to last his lifetime and hers combined.

After requesting another pick-up on the app, she inhaled deeply to calm her nerves and stomach before pushing the doorbell. Sounds came from the other side. Sheridan dared a nervous smile as Norman opened the door.

"Sheridan! What brings you our way?"

She hoped that 'our' didn't mean Noah was there. Just her dumb luck if he was. She considered making a run for it. If only the Lift driver could have stuck around. She took a step backward, forgetting the step down, and went sprawling into the grass.

"Sheridan!" Norman darted out and bent over her. "Are you okay?"

Noah didn't even have to be around to bring out her klutzy side.

"Hi, Norman." Her voice wavered as she got to her feet and brushed herself off. "I think so." Thank goodness she'd changed her mind and wore jeans today instead of that cute sundress.

He frowned at her. "You sure?"

She brushed her hair back from her face. Did she look as red as she felt? "Can I come in for a minute?"

"Of course! Excuse my bad manners. Please, come in."

The faint scent of Noah's cologne hit her as she walked in and intensified the ache in her heart. As she entered the living room, the night of their soup collision came rushing back. As did the memory of their kiss…

Eyes burning, she blinked and turned around to face Norman and pulled an envelope out of her purse. The sooner she did this, the sooner she could leave. "I want you to have this, Norman."

He took the envelope and opened the flap, seeing the check she'd placed inside. "What? Why?"

"To replace at least some of what you lost, thanks to my father. And to thank you for being so kind to me." Her voice wavered again at the end, accompanied by the burn of tears. "Please accept it."

"Sheridan, I can't." He held the envelope toward her. "I told you, you're not responsible for what your father did."

"I know that. I really do. But it would mean a lot to me if you'd keep it."

He glanced down at the check, then returned his gaze to her. "But don't you need this money? When you left you said you were going to stay with your friend."

She gently pushed his hand back. "Part of my trust fund was returned to me. I'll be just fine." She tilted her head. "Please?"

Norman's eyes grew moist. "You're a hard woman to turn down." He put his hand over hers. "I hope it's okay to tell you that I miss you."

She let out a short laugh and hugged him, then drew back. "Of course it is. I miss you too."

He looked into the envelope again. "You know what, this may be just what Noah needs for the restaurant."

"Is he having trouble?" Had Lancaster created more problems for Noah? The thought made her want to box the man in the ears.

Norman's friendly stance turned awkward. "You could kind of say that. Sara's the one who stole that money. I never believed you did it, Sheridan. And neither did Noah."

"He didn't?" Her consolation at being proved innocent didn't compare to her relief in learning that Noah never believed she did it.

"No, he was like a madman trying to find proof. He suspected Sara all along."

As did she, but she'd had no way to prove it. Between her lie of omission and her father's reputation, she hadn't seen the point of trying to convince Noah differently. "What's he going to do now?"

"Noah agreed not to press charges as long Jordan changed his investment into a loan."

"Oh, wow. That's a fair bit of money." How soon would Noah have to make good on that agreement? Even if the lunch seating was a hit, he'd still have to draw in outside resources for that size of a loan.

"He's considering taking a second mortgage on this place, but maybe this will help." He lifted the envelope with his words.

"I'm glad." The thought of the money helping Noah made her feel somehow connected to him still, even if it was tenuous at best. Letting go would take time.

A horn sounded from outside. "That's my ride. You take care of yourself, Norman. And Noah."

He followed her as she headed outside. "Sheridan, where's your car?"

She turned around, glancing at the envelope in his hand.

Recognition dawned in his eyes.

"It was time to let go and move on." She smiled and got in the car, waving as the driver backed out of the drive.

At the end of the street, Sheridan leaned forward. "Can I change the address of my destination?"

"Sure, as long as it's in Sarasota." The woman driving met her gaze in the rearview mirror.

Sheridan gave the woman the address and then pulled

up her bank account on her phone to formulate an exact amount to buy out Jordan Lancaster.

## Chapter Eighteen

Noah picked up his phone from his desk again. No missed calls. No texts either. He'd left several messages for Sheridan and even sent a text to see if she was getting his calls, but she hadn't called or texted him back.

Maybe it was too late. He should have pushed his pride into the garbage disposal and listened to her side of the story in the first place. He'd had enough time to think and had to admit he may have done the same thing in her situation.

And proving she didn't steal that money was just the right thing to do—he knew that. But he still could have called and told her that he didn't believe she did it. Based on what his father told him about their conversation yesterday, Sheridan must have thought he believed Sara.

He still couldn't believe she sold her car. When he got home last night, his father had handed him the envelope with the check, already signed. But Noah had insisted his father keep it, reassured him that he had the restaurant situation covered, which he did. And would.

A knock came from the door. He bounced his gaze up and did a double-take.

Sheridan stood there, dressed in jeans, a purple blouse tied at the waist, and a pair of wedge sandals. She had on the same little earrings she always wore when she swept her hair up like that. And that huge purse hung from her shoulder, as always. She gave him a tentative smile.

"Sheridan." He stood as she walked over to stand in front of his desk, sending his heart into overdrive.

"I hope I'm not catching you at a bad time." Her eyes searched his, dark and questioning.

"No, not at all. It's uh, it's good to see you." Any residual doubts he had flew into the fryer and fizzled away. He'd do whatever it took to win her back. Earn her trust back so she'd see he really wanted her…loved her.

She set her oversized purse on the edge of his desk and pulled out a large envelope. "I have something for you." She hesitated at first but then held out the envelope.

Noah accepted it and slipped out what appeared to be a contractural agreement. He caught Jordan Lancaster's name at first glance, then Sheridan's. He'd been expecting Lancaster's promised documents, but what did Sheridan have to do with their agreement?

"What's this?"

"A gift. To say thank you."

He flipped through the first couple of pages, scanning the text. His father had mentioned something about her getting part of her trust fund, but why would she do this? "Seriously?"

Her laugh was quick and soft. "Yes. You're free of Jordan Lancaster's manipulating interference forever."

He couldn't stop looking at her as his thoughts jumped

from turning her down to accepting her gift. But he had an idea he hoped she'd agree to. "I can't accept this."

Confusion widened those beautiful dark eyes of hers. "But...I thought you'd be relieved."

"Not as a gift, but I can agree to a partnership."

Her lips parted at her surprise, making him want to close the distance between them in the worst way ever. "I thought you didn't want to deal with investors anymore."

"I don't. I'm asking you to be my business partner."

Her expression listed from confusion, appearing more hopeful, but then seemed to slide into something akin to concern. "I'm not sure that's a good idea, Noah."

Had he misread things between them? Had his silence severed his chances with her? He remembered the note she left him. "Sheridan, I'm sorry. I should have listened to your side of the story and been more understanding. And I'm sorry that Sara did that to you. I knew you could never do something like that, because you're right. You are nothing like your father."

She swiped a tear from her cheek and smiled. "Thank you, Noah. I appreciate that. It means a lot to hear you say it."

Right, now he had a potato size lump in his throat. "So what do you say? We work great together. The lunch seating has been a huge success, thanks to you. Madilyn's needs you."

She hesitated at first, then blinked and smiled. "Okay. Deal." She held her hand out.

He shook her hand but loathed letting go of her. The warmth of her skin and proximity to her made him want to throw caution to the wind and pull her into his arms. But he'd do this the right way. Show her how much he not only cared—loved—her but also how much she meant to him.

Everything that made Sheridan unique...she didn't have a clue how amazing she was.

"But I'm not moving back in with you and your father." She laughed.

He knew she meant it as a joke, but he'd be lying if he said he didn't care about that. First, he'd prove to her they could work well together in business. Then he'd convince her they could make a great couple too.

"Dad will be disappointed." He said it as a joke. Well, mostly...but it was true. His father told him he better not let Sheridan get away. And he agreed. He just wasn't sure if she wanted to be caught by him anymore.

---

Having an office space of her own used to be one of her hallmarks of achievement. Now, with a desk butted up against Noah's, she should be happy. She had a great job— not a job, but a partnership in a thriving business. Her father had never promised her anything this lucrative or creative. He probably would have quickly sold the business for the money before passing it down to his daughter. Sadly, she understood her father better now in light of what happened with Sara and now this partnership. And she pitied him more for what he squandered away. He lost his fortune and his family to greed.

But she had to confess—it wasn't enough for her. She wanted to be more than just Noah Kent's business partner. A whole lot more. After three weeks of hoping for some indication that his interest in her—his attraction to her— might be renewed, she had nothing. No clue, no kiss, not even a flirt. The man was positively respectful and nothing more. She'd certainly dropped enough hints.

She laid her head on her arms on the desk. A long day. She'd chalk her frustration up to a day packed full with more clientele than they could seat due to an event featuring local artists. Her role spearheading Madilyn's involvement in the About Town Menu, featuring just about every eatery in downtown Sarasota and a dozen well-known local food trucks had left her drained. She needed a bath and her bed.

"Sheridan, can you come here a minute?" Noah's voice filter into consciousness.

She popped her head up and blinked. Had she dozed off?

Noah leaned into the office doorway with a concerned expression on his face. "You okay?"

"Yeah, sure. What's up?" She stretched and yawned. How fast could she get out of here and get home?

"I need your help in the dining room."

"Okay." Yawning again, she scooted her chair back to stand up with a wobble. As she headed toward the front of the restaurant, she noted the kitchen was dark already. "Did Manny leave already? He promised me he would get those ramekins out for the brunch special."

Noah didn't answer her. Maybe he didn't hear her question. She was too tired to repeat it and her feet hurt. And why was the place so dark?

A click preceded a small burst of flame. The light illuminated Noah's face as he stood over a table and lit a candle in the center. A small table arranged with two place settings sat waiting. The aroma of Margot's pasta carbonara filled her nose as she drew closer and brought an immediate rush of saliva to her mouth. In the rush to manage the food, she'd forgotten to eat some of it.

"What's this?" The candlelight threw dancing shadows across Noah's face but didn't hide his broad smile.

"We're celebrating."

"Celebrating what? Did we get a Michelin Star?" She regretted her sarcasm as soon as his smile dimmed a notch. "Sorry. I'm just tired."

Noah pulled out a chair. "Sit and I'll tell you what we're celebrating." He picked up the bottle of wine sitting on the table and started to fill the glass at the plate intended for her.

Sheridan took a step forward, but her wedge heel caught the carpet and sent her sprawling forward. Right into Noah. The wine bottle tumbled from his hands, landed on the table, and tipped over along with the glass.

Wine splashed all over his shoes and slacks.

"Oh, no!" Sheridan made a grab for the bottle to stop the entire contents from pouring out. Too late for the glass.

How had she done it again? Why could she not be in a room with a wine bottle without spilling the contents everywhere? "Sit. I'll get some towels."

She dashed into the kitchen, popping the light switch on. A stack of freshly laundered bar mops sat by the sink. She grabbed three and started to dash back to the front, but then stopped when she caught sight of the large white salad bowl on the shelf.

After a split-second debate, she grabbed the bowl and hit the faucet.

"Sheridan, where'd you go?"

"Coming!" She walked as quickly as she could without spilling. Her heart raced with her spontaneous plan.

Noah had shed his shoes and was peeling his wine-soaked socks off his feet.

She set the bowl in front of him, then gently nudged one of his feet into the bowl.

"What are doing?" He drew his brows together as he

stared at her with eyes that reminded her of the ocean. And she wanted to swim there forever.

Maybe her plan would convince him that their relationship could be more than business.

After pushing his pant leg out of the way, Sheridan tugged his foot into the bowl—she'd have to buy Chef a new one—and cupped some of the water in her hand to rinse his ankle and lower calf. "The first day I met you, I made a mess. Spilled an expensive bottle of wine all over my feet."

"This one wasn't cheap either." He chuckled.

"Shhh." Candlelight sparkled in his eyes nearly making her forget what she was doing. "You were kind to me, Noah Kent. More kind and caring than anyone had been to me in a long time."

She tugged his other foot into the bowl, pushing the wine-stained pant leg out of the way. *Yet another dry cleaning bill* but she pushed the random thought aside. Once done, she dried his feet and pushed the bowl to the side then sat back on her feet. Gathering every bit of her courage to say what she kept in her heart for weeks, she locked gazes with him. She would accept whatever his reaction was, knowing she'd at least tried.

"I didn't realize…" Her voice wavered with her emotions. She took a deep breath. "I didn't realize until later that I fell in love with you that day. If you feel anything for me…maybe—"

Noah lurched forward, cupping her face between his hands as he crushed his lips against hers. He stood, pulling her up with him, and kissed her again, as if he needed to memorize every part of her lips with his own.

Just as she needed a breath, he pulled back but didn't let go of her face. The candlelight made his eyes look like gems. "I love you too, Sheridan Lane…Scott…whoever you are. I've wanted to tell you for weeks but wanted to regain your trust first."

"My trust? But I'm the one who lied." Was this for real? Never in a million years would she have imagined this.

"You had a good reason. Just don't do it again." His tone teased her, as did his grin that tempted her for a return performance.

She lifted her lips to his for another kiss, wrapping her arms around his back as she pressed against him. Her foot hit the water bowl, sloshing wine water all over her feet and his. She giggled against his mouth, then leaned her head back to assess the mess. "You sure you want in on this piece of work?"

With a low chuckle, he brushed his thumb along her cheek and over her mouth. "I wouldn't want it any other way."

# Chapter Nineteen

"I can't believe I can do this now." He brushed the small tendrils of hair back from her face.

"Do what?" She loved the feel of him, the smell of him, the sound of him...everything. For the first time in a while —perhaps ever—she felt at home, at peace...valued and cherished. How had she wound up with so much after losing everything?

"Kiss you in my office."

Soft laughter rumbled up from her happiness. "Our office."

"Correction. Our office." He lowered his head and kissed her again, long and lingering, as if to make sure the deal they'd made would be sealed forever.

"Um, Boss...Ms. Boss." Manny stood in the doorway with a goofy smile on his face, trying not to look at them.

Noah chuckled but didn't stop staring at her with that love-struck grin she would never tire of. "Yeah?"

"Sorry, didn't mean to interrupt, but that delivery you've been waiting for is here."

He snapped his head around to face Manny. "Oh, right!"

Sheridan bounced her attention between the two of them for some clue of what they were talking about. "What delivery? I don't recall seeing one on the schedule for today."

"That's because this one is a surprise." He grabbed her hand and practically dragged her through the kitchen to the delivery entrance.

First glance told her that was no food delivery truck. The name of the truck, Brett's Electronics & More, gave her a second clue. Then she saw a large box coming out of the back on a dolly. "Nooooo…please tell me you didn't really do this. It's a joke, right?"

After the delivery guy pushed the box off the dolly, Noah walked over to it, patted the top, and sported a proud smile. "We are now the proud owners of The Singing Machine—"

"Yeah, I get it. A karaoke machine." She put her hand on one hip and gestured with her other hand. "But I told you this doesn't fit Madilyn's image."

His grin couldn't get any bigger or win her heart over more. "This is a professional-level machine. Compact, no big screen needed. We hold special events on the patio and private parties."

She dropped her arm and closed the distance between them. "So no Friday night karaoke."

He paused. "Not right away."

She poked his stomach. "No, I firmly protest."

He pulled her into his arms and kissed her senses silly. "Are you sure about that?"

She touched his lips. "Keeping doing that and you might convince me otherwise."

Noah sat in his usual booth, surrounded by his spreadsheets. Only now they were legit print outs and not his hand written versions. He'd protested at first, but Sheridan had persuaded him over time to make the switch.

He had to admit. She was right. Less time spent figuring things out manually.

And numbers didn't lie. The restaurant was in a steady growth pattern with an upward turn that started several months ago—around the time Sheridan stepped into the place and into his life.

If there were such a thing as a spreadsheet of his life, the numbers would be the same. He chuckled at the thought.

"What are you laughing about now?" Sheridan slid into the booth across from him and spun the spreadsheet around to face her.

"Nothing. Just thinking."

"About what?" She studied the page with her usual precision. Part of why they'd seen so much growth in the place.

He could add himself to her list of accomplishments. The woman had radically changed his life for the better. His father's too. "About you."

She lifted her gaze to his and smiled. "Do tell."

"You're amazing, you know that, right?"

Tears welled in the bottom of her eyes. "I'm glad you think so."

"Dad does too."

Sheridan nodded and blinked, which knocked the tears loose. She swiped her hands across her cheeks. "You're making a mess of me."

He'd tried to figure out the right time and place to do this for almost a month now. This moment and in the booth where they had their first encounter hit the mark better than anything he could have planned.

Noah reached into his pocket for the small pouch holding the ring he'd carried around since the day he bought it. He slipped the ring out and held it up.

Sheridan's eyes opened wide to match the circle of her perfect lips. "Are you? Me? Asking?"

He loved the way she fumbled her words whenever she got nervous or excited. "Yes, Sheridan Lane Scott. I'm asking. We make outstanding partners in business. I'd like to make it permanent in life as well. Will you marry me?"

She shot out of her side of the booth and into his. "You better believe I will."

After he slipped the ring on her finger, she slammed him with a kiss that left no doubt about her feelings. Good thing the restaurant wasn't open yet.

She drew back, still cupping his face in her hands. Tears streamed down her cheeks. "Now you're really making a mess of me."

He ran his thumb across one cheek to swipe the tears away. "That's okay. I'm really good at cleaning up."

# Epilogue

"I just love how you set this all up, Sheri!" Kaleena swept her hand to encompass the full patio set up with cafe lights zigzagged overhead, a smattering of cafe tables and benches, and a small stage at the back end. Dusk had fallen, bringing out the first hint of stars and a light breeze that rustled the palms.

"I know, right?!? I love this space."

Kaleena hugged her. "And I can't think of a better way to break it in than your engagement party."

Tears blurred her vision as she stepped back and let Kaleena's joy wash over her. How had she gone from losing everything, including her family for the most part, to gaining a true "framily" of trusted friends whom she adored and stood by her?

So unexpected.

"To be honest, I'm overwhelmed by it, but in a good way. I never dreamed...never imagined this could be my life."

Kaleena squeezed her hand. "And yet it is, and here we

are." She chuckled as she swung her gaze over the small gathering. "Where's Noah? I want to congratulate him, too."

Sheridan spun around and found him standing near the karaoke stand, talking to Emma. Manny walked over and joined them.

"Oh, will you look at that?" Kaleena looked like a kid who had just discovered chocolate milkshakes for the first time.

Sheridan searched for some clue of what had grabbed Kaleena's fascination. "What?"

Kay gave her a quick glance. "Don't you see the sparks flying between those two?"

Her gut twisted into a knot. "Noah and Emma?"

"No!" Kay swatted her lightly. "Noah is so deep into you, I'm amazed he can still walk. I mean Manny and that cute blonde next to him."

"That cute blonde is Emma. We've been best friends since college."

"She's not one of those who snubbed you, I hope."

"No, Emma was my only friend for a while…until I crashed into your place."

Kay let loose a giggle. "Oh, I never tire of revisiting Miss Snooty Pants."

"Yeah, don't think I haven't noticed." Sheridan laughed with her.

Noah did a small double-take when he noticed she was staring at him, then disengaged and walked toward her.

"I gotta say, Sheri, that is one fine man you've landed there."

"Yes, he is. Sometimes I still wonder how he fell for me."

"Oh, he's as blessed as you are, honey. Don't you ever

forget that. You two were designed for each other, no doubt there."

Noah slipped his arm around her waist. "You two look like you're up to something."

Kay sported a mock innocent expression. "Us? No, never. But we are observing some interesting chemistry happening there between Manny and Emma."

Noah nodded. "I noticed a little something happening there, too." He dropped his ocean blue eyes to hers. "Is Emma attached?"

Sheridan shook her head. "Nothing serious at the moment." She hesitated to say more out of respect for her friend, whose heart seemed to get broken on a regular basis.

Sheridan continued to study the pair as they approached the karaoke machine. "How cute. They're going to do a song together."

Noah blew out a breath. "Manny's moving fast."

Sheridan had never seen Manny be anything but sweet and caring, but she didn't like what Noah wasn't saying. "Do I need to warn Emma about Manny?"

A battle between ratting out his friend and being honest with his fiancée pushed his expression into a tortured frown. "Um, well, Manny can be a player sometimes."

"Oh, no…this is so not good. Emma falls hard and fast." Sheridan waited for the song to end and then cringed when Manny went in for a kiss on her cheek.

And there it was. She knew that look. Emma would take that and run with it all the way to a wedding shop if she could. "Oh, this is so not good."

Noah tugged her closer. "Manny seems genuinely interested. Things could work out."

She breathed a sigh of relief when Calen approached the karaoke stage. He'd keep an eye on Emma.

Sheridan looked up at Noah. "Can I hold you to that?"

"As in a deal?" His voice turned low and teasing. "What are the terms?"

"Lifetime."

He captured her lips in a slow kiss, then drew back. "I accept."

Next in the Seashells and Sunsets series

vinci-books.com/friendlydisaster

**When love hides in plain sight, will it bloom or fade away?**

Calen Cooper has spent a lifetime hiding how he feels about his best friend. But when Emma finally finds a relationship that isn't a total train wreck, Calen sees the door closing on any chance of them being more than friends.

Turn the page for a free preview…

# The Friendly Disaster: Chapter One

Prussian blue had to be a gift from the art gods.

Which said a lot considering she didn't care for most shades of blue. Even the blue of her own eyes could use a little Prussian blue so they didn't look so pale. But she adored shades of olive green, peridot, mustard yellow, burnt orange, rust red...

So many colors, so little time.

Emma Price dipped her brush into a small dab of the expensive watercolor she'd allotted herself for this project. Her salary as a part-time teacher at the art college barely made ends meet, let alone allowed for watercolor paint that ran close to twenty bucks for a small tube.

She supplemented by teaching private art classes at her art studio in a refurbished warehouse not far from Pineapple Avenue, which mostly covered her student loans.

The price for living in a beach town.

Totally. Worth. It.

She touched her brush to the watercolor paper she'd

prepped and melted into the glorious gradation of color. The deeper tones captured the blue jay's feathers almost to perfection, without having to adjust the color much at all. And though she considered her piece an abstract representation, she wanted to capture the essence of these fierce creatures.

Fierce, that is, to the squirrels who tried to steal their food from the feeder she'd hung from her small apartment balcony, and to any other bird trying to fly in for a meal. She could relate—she'd spent her lunch money on a tube of paint.

Again, totally worth it.

She sighed as she dragged the brush across the paper, building the layers of the feathers. The lighter areas had a gray-blue touch that still maintained the richness of the color.

"That was quite a sigh."

Emma jumped in her seat, which jerked her hand and left an obnoxious blue blob jutting from the feather she'd just meticulously painted. She growled and grabbed a paper towel to dab up the color before it set.

"Sorry. I didn't mean to startle you." Calen tucked his hands in the top of his jean pockets and slumped his shoulders. "That blue is intense."

"Prussian blue, and I love it." She caught most of the bleed, and could probably fix the rest after it dried. Watercolors were not as forgiving as acrylics and oils. "What are you doing here, Calen? How did you know where I was?"

"Because this is your happy place. Besides, Sheridan told me you'd be in your studio working today."

"You sabotaged my best friend?" She tossed the paper towel at the can and missed.

Calen picked up the wad and dropped it into the

garbage. "You wouldn't return my texts. Or my call. And what am I? Aren't I your best friend?"

She swished the paintbrush off in the nearby cup of water, dried it on a cloth, and then ran the bristles over her tongue to hold them together before she stuck the wooden end into the bun on top of her head—her way of keeping track of her brushes. Especially the small ones. Though sometimes she still forgot and found several stuck in there.

"Sheridan's my best friend, who's a *girl*. You're my best friend, who's a *guy*."

"Thank you for that delineation. I'm glad I'm still your *best* friend." He dodged her gaze, showing more interest in her painting.

Delineation? She hadn't heard that one yet. He must have spent the morning researching words for his poetry. "Just barely. After that performance last night, you almost slipped into the just-a-friend category."

The memory had played through her mind over and over. A perfect party to celebrate Sheridan and Noah's engagement. Singing karaoke with Manny, who'd seemed like a great guy. Super cute too. And a sous chef at Madilyn's Grill & Wine Bar. Then Calen's lunge at the platform, fist flying through the air and connecting with Manny's beautifully chiseled jaw. And down he went.

Manny, that is.

Calen had stood there looking like a misguided Viking. She had to say that seeing him that impassioned had surprised...maybe even impressed her at first, but then the horrific realization of what he'd done took over.

Now her chances with Manny were likely ruined, thanks to Calen's presumptuous attempt to protect her.

"I tried to apologize, but you took off." He fiddled with

her paint tubes, lining them up in a neat row so the labels faced upward.

"I'm not the one you should apologize to. Manny's the one sporting a sore jaw today, thanks to you."

"Did you talk to him?"

Did he sound hopeful or worried? She swiveled back to her painting. "No. I'm not sure he wants to talk to me after that debacle." There. She threw one of her own recent discoveries at him. *Debacle*. She'd had to look up how to pronounce it, though.

"Great word." He held his hands out. "I tried to apologize to him, but he'd left by the time I got back from trying to find you." Hands tucked back into his jean pockets, he shrugged. "I'm sorry. I thought he was that guy who dumped you last week."

"Well, he wasn't."

"Yeah, I know that now. Sheridan elucidated."

After an eye roll at yet another one of his new words, she studied him for a moment, this quirky guy she'd known since middle school. They'd shared almost as much life together as apart. She rose from her seat and rested her hands on his shoulders. "I know, and I appreciate it, but you really don't have to defend my honor, or whatever Shakespearean term you choose to call it. And I like the hair, by the way."

"Gets in my face a lot." He ran his hands through both sides to push it back, only to have it fall back in front of his eyes. He blew at it to make a point.

She touched the bottom of his hair just below his ears. "Just a little longer and you can tie it into a man-bun. Then you'll really look like a poet."

He rolled his eyes at her. "We'll see if I can stand it that lo—"

"Am I interrupting?" Manny stood in the doorway. His chef's jacket hung open, revealing a snug black T-shirt that tucked rather well into a pair of black sports pants. Better than she remembered from last night...

She'd better snap her chin back in place before she drooled. "Uh, hi!" The last word sounded more like a squeak toy. She cleared her throat. "Hi, Manny. This is a surprise."

Calen drew his brows together at her formal words. She sent him her signal that told him to back off. The one they'd established in high school to let the other know not to approach because they were in flirt mode. Calen said hers reminded him of a mad chipmunk.

Whatever, didn't matter. Just so long as he got the message.

Manny darted his gaze from her to Calen, then back to her. "Am I? Interrupting?"

She broke into a full smile and blinked—something she'd learned early on drew attention to her blue eyes even if they weren't dark enough to be considered compelling. "No, not at all. How'd you find me?"

"I asked Sheridan. Hope you don't mind. I really wanted to see you again." His voice lowered with his last sentence, sending a warm sensation through her. And he kept staring at her as if she rocked his world.

"Remind me to smack, then thank Sheridan." She said it more to herself than anything.

"What?" Calen and Manny asked at the same time, which made them frown at each other.

With a forced laugh, she waved it off. Why so nervous? Was she still breathing? Still standing? Her heart beat so loud in her ears that she couldn't tell. *Oh, no no no...not now.*

An anxiety attack would totally blow her chances with Manny. "I think I'll sit down."

"Breathe, Emma." Calen crouched in front of her, his face a blanket of calm concern. "Look at me and just breathe."

He knew better than anyone how random her attacks could be and how to help her head them off. But she didn't want him drawing attention to it either. She did what he said...deep breath...exhale...kept her eyes focused on the flecks of olive green in his hazel eyes. The tightness in her chest released and her breathing normalized.

"I'm fine, Calen." She gave him her look again. He was blocking her view of Manny. Dark and mysterious Manny, as she thought of and pictured him in her mind. He'd mentioned something about his father being Portuguese and his mother Italian. Made for the perfect mix of tall, dark, and handsome.

"Got it." He backed up a step and faced Manny. "Hey, about last night..."

Manny took Calen's place in front of her. "Not a problem. Sheridan explained everything." He didn't even look away when he answered Calen. Just kept examining her with that concerned expression.

Calen bobbed his head forward, which made him look like an awkward chicken. "Good. Still, I'm sorry I punched you."

Manny shot him a stern glance. "Like I said, not a problem."

The man should be on a magazine cover. How did GQ not know about him? Or some restaurant industry magazine? There must be one that he'd be the perfect cover material for.

He took her hand. "Are you okay?"

"All good. Thanks. Probably just dehydrated from my walk this morning." The warmth of his hand made her melt more than Prussian blue. That had to be something, right? Were they meant to be? She'd definitely sacrifice her pricey paints for this guy.

No doubt about it.

He rose to his full height, which turned out to be a few inches taller than her and almost as tall as Calen, yet his presence made him seem taller. The man knew how to fill a room. "What are you working on?"

"Oh, just a practice piece, really. Something I plan to demonstrate to my class." She lifted the pad. "Where is my paintbrush?"

"In your hair." Calen was still here? Why did he sound irritated? Didn't he catch her signal?

"I didn't know you taught too." Manny tugged it from her bun and held it out to her. "Can I watch you paint?"

"Of course!" She slid over on the seat and patted the space she'd made.

Calen's sigh came from somewhere behind her. "Catch you later, Emma."

"Later, Calen!" She tossed her reply over her shoulder, which brought her face closer to Manny's. His musky scent filled her senses and took her breath away.

She exhaled and gave herself a mental shake as she picked up her favorite paint tube. "This is one of my faves—it's called Prussian blue."

---

He'd give it two weeks. Three at the most.

Calen Cooper had a knack for predicting the length of Emma's relationships. Of course, years of practice had trained him well. Emma had a habit of falling for the wrong guys.

Shiny at first, then gone.

None of her relationships seemed to last long despite her intense desire for happily-ever-after. He had a theory why but kept it to himself. Any mention of Emma's father shut her down faster than a bad metaphor made him want to puke. Her real father, that is.

Calen had met the man only a few times when he and Emma hung out in middle school. Then her parents divorced, which started the panic attacks for Emma. Her father didn't know how to deal with them, so she saw him less and less until he finally stopped calling at all.

And despite having a fantastic stepfather by the time high school came, Emma never quite shook the rejection. Or the panic attacks. Over time, she'd learned to manage them better until they didn't happen very often. Only when she got overwhelmed or badly stressed out, but painting was her best remedy.

He wandered down the hall, passing several other artist studios. Felt bizarre not being at his coffee shop, but even business owners needed days off. And he'd promised himself that he'd work on his poetry today, which he did. Researched a list of words to add to his 'poetic vocabulary,' as Emma liked to call it. He preferred *expanding his mind*.

At the end of the hall, he turned into Maverick's Metal Studio, one of the larger units in an old renovated warehouse redesigned into various sized studios and marketed as 'workspaces empowered for the creative at heart.'

He hated bad personifications. "Hey, Mav."

Maverick stood over a large worktable with his welding helmet pushed up on his head, examining the tip of a welding torch. "Hey, Calen, what's up?"

"Came to check on Emma. Figured I'd come by and see if you have my order ready."

Mav gave him a questioning look. "I heard there was some commotion last night at Madilyn's."

Pineapple Avenue news traveled fast. "Heard about that, huh?"

"Yeah, heard you punched some guy out." Mav's grin of approval should make him feel somewhat vindicated, but it didn't. Just more of an idiot.

"Seems I punched the wrong guy."

After putting the torch down, Mav slipped off his heavy-duty gloves and leaned a jean-clad hip against the workbench. "She seems to pick the wrong guy a lot."

"Yeah, she has a type. Tall, dark, and trouble."

Mav's studious expression shifted into a lopsided grin, which raised his dark brow on that side.

Calen shook his head. "Don't even think about it."

He chuckled as he shifted to face his workbench again. "Don't worry. I don't date artists. Too much drama."

Such irony. How could he resist? "And yet, you are one." He flourished his hand outward for emphasis like a model at a cheesy car show.

"Not exactly. When your tool is a welding torch, you're considered a craftsman. Besides, I make practical stuff too. As you know." He leaned over the workbench and pulled up a metal display rack. "I followed your specs to the letter."

"Great! Thanks." Calen slipped out his wallet and pulled out their agreed amount.

Mav reached over again and lifted a rod that had hooks on each end and the word *breathe* in script, forming the middle. "And this."

He'd asked Mav to create the hanger for Emma's bird feeder. "That came out great. What do I owe you?"

"Fifty. You know, you could have just bought something like that for less."

"But then it wouldn't be an original."

Mav grabbed a magazine off the side desk and flopped it open in front of Calen. A picture very similar to the one Mav had made stared at him. And at half the price. "I used it for reference. See? Practical."

Calen pulled out more bills and handed them to him. "Yes, but this one won't say *Made by Mav*." He looked upward, imagining the label.

Mav screwed up his face like he'd just eaten a bad shrimp. "Dude."

"Yeah, that sounded way better in my head." But he did have a question. "Is Maverick your first or last name?"

No lopsided Mav-smile this time. "Yes."

Calen took a moment to process that one. "Okay then."

After stuffing the money into his pocket, Mav pointed at him. "You know, you would be a good fit for Emma."

He flattened his hands on his chest as he recoiled back. "Me? No way. We've known each other for too long. I had a crush on her back in high school, but that's ancient history."

"But you're the only one who seems to really get that girl, Calen. You gotta admit, she's a hot mess."

With extenuating circumstances. "But she's also super smart and creative. She just needs someone to complement her weaknesses, that's all. And protect her."

"Sure that's not you?"

"Trust me. I couldn't be more certain."

# The Friendly Disaster: Chapter Two

The first glimmers of dawn promised a sunny day and the cool temperature a mildly humid one. Typical for Florida this time of year, as summer crept closer. Perfect beach weather too.

Calen read the sign displayed in the art gallery window. With the arrival of a major designer shopping mall a few years back, many strip malls had converted deserted spaces into art galleries. When the last place in this spot failed last year, the owners brought in a gallery to fill the space as a temporary solution. Who knew The Pineapple Avenue Art Gallery would become such a thriving success, giving their section of downtown Sarasota even more foot traffic and credence throughout the area? Even off-season, which they'd soon enter on the other side of Easter.

But this was a first—an official art show dedicated to local artists sponsored by two major art galleries in New York and LA.

*Local artists are invited to submit portfolios for this prestigious show...well-known art critics...select pieces will continue to be featured in the NY and LA galleries...*

He had to tell Emma. She should do this. She needed to do this. She *deserved* this.

And she would do it too, wouldn't she? Unlike him, who never went beyond publishing his poetry in neat little booklets he created on his own laser printer. And only sold them out of his coffee shop, which most who frequented Java Jerry's weren't really looking for poetry. Kaleena had sold a couple in her shop, Sass & Sun. Tourists loved her place even more than the locals.

Safe. That was his MO when it came to his art. But Emma...even in her messiness, she was fierce and bold. Two things he'd always loved about her. She should totally go for this.

Carrying the metal display rack and Emma's hanger he'd picked up from Mav yesterday, he crossed the street to his shop and went in through the front door. The early morning business crowd in need of caffeine would converge soon, leaving him just enough time to get this display up. He had a new line of teas he suspected would be the new rage with new agers and health nuts.

*New rage with new age...* The words danced into a rhyme in his head as he prepped the espresso machine and started a fresh round of coffee pots brewing.

So many words, so little time.

He finished setting up the tea display. The cardamon chai was his favorite so far. He read the packaging slogan again, "Time for tea and tea is time." Calen rolled his eyes with a groan.

A giggle drew his attention. How had he missed Emma's entrance?

"There's another revenue stream for you, Calen. Write better product slogans."

"Not on your life. That's why I opened this lucrative business of selling coffee and tea until I'm a famous poet."

"That's right. And when is that supposed to happen? Have you added it to your spreadsheet yet?"

He shot her a dirty look. "There is nothing wrong with setting goals."

She stood next to him and laid her head against his shoulder. "I agree, but goals can't be reached if you don't try. And they say if you write them down, you're more likely to go after them. Sounds right up your alley...writing things down. Did you submit to that poetry magazine you love?"

Her bun, which she called her blonde bomb, tickled under his neck. And she must have changed shampoo... patchouli and vanilla.

He grabbed a packet of chai tea. "I want you to try this tea and tell me what you think of it. I'll brew you a cup right now." He could feel her stare drilling into him as he darted behind the counter.

She sighed. "Fine, I won't push. But you know I'm right. You need to go for it, Calen. You're too good to stay hidden."

"Speaking of displaying your work, did you see the sign on the gallery window next door?"

"Are you kidding? It's all I hear about on campus. Even the students are discussing their submissions. There's going to be a lot of competition and a lot of grumpy students as the deadline nears. I am not looking forward to that. They're still hormonal teenagers to some degree. That's just adding fire to turpentine."

He smiled and pointed at her. "Nice imagery association there."

She gave him her best smile, the one that highlighted the light dusting of freckles on her cheeks. "I thought you'd like that one."

"Well, are you going to submit?"

She dropped her gaze. "Me? I don't know. Haven't really thought about it."

Her voice dropped as she spoke, which meant she was lying. And hiding.

"You were born for this, Emma. That gallery won't have displayed true art until your work is up there."

She did a laugh-snort combo as she looked at him. Her eyes held that glimmer of fear that going for it might come at a cost of her carefully managed peace and tranquility. "I guess I'll think about it."

He put a top on the to-go cup and slid it across the counter to her. "Promise me you'll think about it. And I'll help you with whatever you need so you don't get over-whelmed."

She gave him a noncommittal nod before lifting the cup and inhaled. "This smells amazing. Thanks." She glanced at her phone. "I better get going."

He called out as she headed to the door. "Let's talk more later. It's movie night."

She didn't look back as she pushed through the door. "Can't. Have a date."

He'd planned to give her the hanger he'd had made for her tonight. Guess that would have to wait, too.

---

What did she just read?

Emma flipped back a page and started the chapter again. At this rate, she'd finish the book next year. Maybe she should just give up. Her mind seemed more content to replay the story of her afternoon painting with Manny.

After glancing at her watch and noting the meager fifteen minutes she had left to soak in some sun to keep her vitamin D level up before her next class, she dropped the novel into her bag and relaxed, eyes closed, and let her mind explore the Manny Memories, as she liked to call them.

This mental album was filling up faster than the norm with cataloged details, too. She loved his smile. He swore he never had braces, yet every time he grinned, she thought of her zinc oxide paint and how much fun she'd have painting his gorgeous teeth. So white and perfect. And such a contrast to his dark complexion and black hair.

And his smell. Even through the lingering odors of the restaurant on his jacket, she caught the scent of his soap—lavender with a touch of patchouli. But then he took his jacket off, revealing a very well-developed physique—that she replayed a couple more times. How did he manage to look that good when he was around food *all the time*?

*Breathe, Emma.*

Calen's voice in her head interrupted the Manny Memories. She needed to take a breath and slow her heart down. Otherwise, she'd scare this one off, too. Just like the last one…*Chaaaarles*. The one time she had a panic attack while dating him, he'd told her to calm down. And not in a compassionate way. More like annoyed. She'd told him to have a wonderful evening dining alone and left the restaurant.

No surprise he didn't call her again.

She mentally pictured herself pulling that album off the shelf and pitching it into a large garbage can. And burning it. She laughed.

"What's so funny?"

Looking up, Emma cracked open an eye against the sun. Nina stood over her. Too bad she wasn't just a smidge taller so she'd block the sun about to blind her. "Just reflecting on the past."

Nina plopped down on the bench next to Emma, letting the tote bag on her shoulder slide to the sidewalk with a thump. "Is this day over yet?"

"I thought Mondays were your favorite day of the week?"

"I've decided to join forces with the world and hate them." Nina poked her bottom lip out for emphasis. "Everything was fine until they asked me to fill in for Professor Dumbledore."

Emma giggled. She loved the way Nina called the other instructors by movie character names. "Who's he again?"

"You know, Mr. Winston. He's originally from *Engggglaaand*. White hair and beard. Wears a funny hat sometimes." Her expression turned deadpan.

"I don't think I've met him yet. So what's the problem?"

"I don't enjoy teaching the fine art classes."

"But that's what your degree is in."

"Yes, but I like the film classes better." She let out a long breath and then smiled. "It'll be fine. What's new in your world, Ms. Price Is Right?"

Emma rolled her eyes. Nina spent too much time in TV land. "Oh, perhaps a Mr. Right."

"Seriously? You've only been dating that guy for like two weeks." Nina gave her a look of disbelief.

"No, not that guy. This one I just met. Well, kind of. I've noticed him before when I went into Madilyn's to see Sheridan, but then he started noticing me at her engagement party."

"Wasn't that just last weekend?"

"I know, but Manny is marvelous." Calen would be proud of her alliteration. "He dropped by my studio yesterday." She put her hand over Nina's wrist. "He actually asked Sheridan where he could find me. Can you believe he sought me out like that?"

Nina tilted her head. "He sounds amazing, but what happened to the other guy?"

"Charles? Oh, that didn't work out. Seems he can't handle dating a woman who has sporadic anxiety attacks."

This time Nina put her hand over Emma's and frowned. "I'm so sorry. He sounds like a jerk."

The thought of him still stung a bit, and she'd only watched half a day's worth of Mr. Bean this time. So maybe that meant she'd been more in love with the idea of Charles and not Charles himself? He'd certainly shown his true colors.

Or maybe she just wanted to live the dream, like Sheridan was. Met Prince Charming, fell in love, nearly lost him, and now was about to live her happily ever after with a magical wedding in a few months.

*Swoooooooooon*...sigh...just like the movies...

"It's fine. I'm fine." She waved her hand at Nina as she looked away. No need to let her see the waterworks threatening in her eyes. At some point, she had to learn how to pick the right guy, one who didn't think of her panic attacks as a defect. She'd certainly had enough practice looking. And she had it on good authority that her heart had put in a transfer request if it happened again.

Manny had to be the one. Had to be.

# The Friendly Disaster: Chapter Three

What will it be like dining at a restaurant with a chef?

She hadn't thought about it until they walked into the restaurant. Will Manny critique the food the entire time, the way Calen critiqued package descriptions in the grocery store? Of course, he only did that to make her laugh.

But this place seemed more upscale than Madilyn's. Clean lines and lots of windows brought the view of the Gulf inside as part of the setting. Very mid-century modern in its design.

The hostess led them to a booth that overlooked a walkway leading to the dock. A profusion of plants filled oversized planters situated in the middle of the decking below. The entire scene made her inhale deeply and then exhale. A layer of her stressful week sloughed off like a bad sunburn.

"Great view." She tore her gaze from the incredible scenery to look at Manny.

"I agree." The twinkle in his eyes told her he meant her.

He reached across the table and held her hand. "I'm glad you like it. I love this place."

He kept smiling at her too, with his big, bright white smile. Was this how Kate Bosworth's character felt in *Win a Date with Tad Hamilton*? Manny certainly gave Josh Duhamel a run for his money. She'd gladly play Rosalee to his Tad any day.

"You have an amazing smile." The words flooded out in a gush of emotion before she could stop herself.

"Thank you. So do you." He released her hand to touch her face. "I love your freckles."

Emma did a sharp intake and felt her cheeks grow warm. She hadn't been out in the sun enough today to get burned, so it was all him. None of her past relationships had started out this smoothly. Was Manny as enamored with her as she was with him?

Calin's voice sounded in her head again. *Breathe, Emma.*

She smiled to mask her inhale, then exhaled just as their server came to the table. Manny asked several questions about the specials, which gave her a few minutes to recompose herself. If she didn't pace herself, she'd pass out before they finished their meal and blow her chances with him.

Manny settled back into his side of the booth with one arm stretched out on the back of the seat. "So, Emma...tell me more about yourself."

She loved the way her name rolled off his lips, the way the 'a' lingered on his tongue, giving just a hint of his bilingual heritage. And the brief pause he allowed before his next word; as if he were savoring the sound of her name.

"Well, I paint." She let out a nervous laugh. "But you already know that. I teach classes part-time at the local art college and privately as well."

He leaned forward. "Private lessons?"

"Yes, small classes. The project I was working on yesterday is for one of those."

"What other kinds of art do you teach?"

"Mostly fine art classes at the college. Privately, it varies. Landscape painting, figure drawing—"

"Figure drawing? You mean like nudes? You must use models, right?"

"Sometimes, or my students take turns drawing each other if I can't find a model. Uh, with their clothes on, that is." Another nervous laugh. She swallowed. "I didn't want you to think anything weird was going on."

He leaned forward as he brought her hand to his lips and kissed her fingers just below her knuckle line. "I've never posed for an artist. Sounds like…fun."

Her heart hit the floor, bounced, and stuck to the ceiling like a wet noodle. The man made her weak in the knees. Good thing they were sitting. "Well, that would certainly be interesting."

"I'm serious. I'd be happy to be your model." He smiled. "And with clothes on."

Did she just burst into flames? Or had management turned off the air conditioning?

She picked up her menu and fanned herself. "Our server keeps looking over to see if we're ready to order."

"Oh, right." He let go of her hand and picked up his menu.

Emma hadn't actually seen their server looking, but she imagined that was the case. Manny certainly knew how to match her intensity. So unexpected…

She scanned down the menu and picked the first dish that jumped out at her, then peeked over the top to study

Manny's face again. His expression had turned serious as he studied the selection. Dark brows dipped into a V-shape above the most beautifully shaped nose she'd ever seen on a man. His well-defined lips pursed against the finger he held against his mouth in thought. And then his jaw. Though a tad cliché, sculpted fit the bill. Her mind became a canvas as she imagined how she'd paint him.

He glanced up and smiled when he caught her staring at him and then quirked one brow up as if to tease her. He certainly knew how to flirt with the best of them. What did a guy like him see in a girl like her, anyway?

He was definitely model material, and she definitely was not.

Calen moved the container in slow circles under the steamer wand to maximize the froth. Chai tea latte with extra cardamom. Not cinnamon. Kaleena's standing order. Since the coffee shop tended to be slow until after the early dinner crowd turned into dessert and coffee foot traffic, he'd decided to make Kaleena's order early and bring it over to her himself.

Something he did occasionally, but on this one, he had an agenda. He needed some wisdom. And the 4-1-1 on Manny.

After dusting the top with cardamon, he snapped a cover on the disposable coffee cup. He waved Steph over to take over the counter. "Be right back."

"Sure thing." She took her station behind the register as if ready for someone to magically appear in front of her. Couldn't fault her for her determination. And since he'd hired her three months ago, Steph had turned into his most reliable employee.

Crossing Pineapple Avenue between crosswalks this time of day wasn't hard. But he did do his due diligence to make sure there weren't any retired snowbirds backing out of the parking spaces. The narrow street sometimes threw them for a loop.

When he walked into Sass & Sun Fashions, he did a quick inventory of the store. Empty at the moment. Maybe Kay would have time for a chat after all…

She looked up from the register. "Well, hey there, neighbor."

He held her cup up. "Shop was slow, so I thought I'd bring it over for you."

"You are a Godsend, Calen Cooper." She picked up her drink, inhaled, and sighed.

"Rough day?"

She took a sip and *mmmed*. "Not anymore."

He gave a small bow. "Glad to be of service."

"Much appreciated." She picked up a couple of items and walked over to one of her shelves. "Something on your mind?"

"What makes you ask?"

She turned around and pointed at him. "That expression. Usually means you're chewing on something. So cough it up." She snorted at her own pun.

He tried not to moan. And failed. "That the best you can do?"

"Considering the day I've had? Yes. So get to it."

He gave a sheepish glance toward her dressing rooms. "This one may require some ottoman time."

She broke into a full grin. "I'll put up my sign."

Calen made his way to the back area as Kay put her 'closed for 15 minutes' sign up and locked the door.

The oversized olive green ottoman in the middle of the changing room area had a bit of a reputation on Pineapple Avenue. First, because the previous shop owner died on it, which Kay didn't find out until she bought the space, and then had it thoroughly cleaned. Now the changing area not only served her customers but also the occasional business neighbor in need of advice.

Kaleena Brooks was a whiz at advice.

And sometimes a little insider information, which was what he needed today.

He dropped onto the soft velvet cushion and leaned his forearms on his knees.

Kay sat down next to him. "Ok, spill it."

"Man, you are full of bad metaphors today."

She arched a finely drawn brow at him. "Says the beggar who's being choosey with his fifteen minutes."

He ran his hands through his hair before standing up. "It's about Emma."

Kay shot him a side-long glance. "What about her?"

"More specifically, it's about Manny. She's dating him."

"Sheridan mentioned something about that."

Calen rushed to sit back down next to Kay. "What do you know about him?"

She shrugged. "Not much, really. Sheridan did mention he can be a player at times but thinks highly of him. And he's always very polite when I come in to pick up my orders. Seems like an all-around nice guy."

"So, he dates a lot of women?"

She barked a laugh. "Honey, you'd have to ask him that." She patted his knee. "Why are you so concerned? Is something going on between you and Emma?"

"No. Not at all. She's my best friend, and I'm trying to look out for her."

"Like you did at Sheridan's engagement party?"

He stood, rubbing the back of his neck. "That was just a misunderstanding. I apologized to both of them. Emma understands I was trying to protect her."

Kay turned her head and narrowed her right eye in question. "Are you sure that's all it was?"

"Of course. What else would it be?" First Mav, now Kay? Why all of a sudden did his friendship with Emma seem under examination?

She raised her brows at him. "You tell me."

He shook his head. "Nothing to tell. We've been friends for years. I just want to make sure she doesn't get her heart wrecked again."

"Again?"

"Yeah, she falls fast and then hard when the guy dumps her." Or she dumps him because he can't deal with her panic attacks.

"Oh, I'm sorry to hear that. She's blessed to have a friend like you in her life. Maybe she just needs some help to understand what kind of guy is right for her."

Why was Kay studying him like that? Seriously? "Yeah, maybe…"

She did a little hop as she shifted on the ottoman. Excitement lit up her eyes. "Let me ask you this. What if Manny turns out to be the one?"

Now there was a question he hadn't expected. "The one…"

"You know. *The One*. Will you be okay with not being the only man in her life?"

Yeah, he knew what she meant, but he hadn't really considered that angle. "Of course. She's had boyfriends in the past, and they seemed fine with our friendship."

"But has she had any long-term relationships?"

He paused. "Nothing longer than a few weeks. She seems to have a type. And I have my theories on that."

"Which are?"

Should he share something that personal about Emma?

"Calen, you know I would never share anything you tell me in confidence, but I also don't want you to feel pressured to tell me something that's none of my business."

He ran a hand over his mouth. "Emma's parents divorced just before we became friends in middle school. By high school, her mother had remarried and Emma considered her stepfather her dad. But sometimes she still struggled with it, especially on her birthday."

"Did her father not keep in contact?"

"He tried at first, then just stopped calling. Sometimes she would imagine he was a CIA agent and had to *go dark* to protect his family." He did air quotes for emphasis.

Kay made a *tsking* sound. "Poor kid. That kind of rejection can steer a person's life."

Calen nodded. "When she showed me a picture of him a few years back, the pieces fell in place."

"The guys she dates are like him?"

"Yep, tall, dark, and never stick around."

"So she's seeking her father's acceptance over and over again. Have you ever brought this up to her?"

"No, I'm not sure how, to be honest. It's a touchy subject."

Kay pushed herself up and patted him on the shoulder. "Like I said, she's blessed to have a friend like you in her life."

"I suppose."

"I'm going to keep that sweet girl in my prayers." Kay pointed at him. "And sometimes people don't realize what—or who—they need most is standing right in front of them."

**Grab your copy...**
**vinci-books.com/friendlydisaster**